DRILLED

POWERTOOLS: THE ORIGINAL CREW RETURNS, BOOK 2

JAYNE RYLON

HAPPY ENDINGS PUBLISHING

V2

eBook ISBN: 978-1-947093-17-1

Print ISBN: 978-1-947093-18-8

Cover Design by Jayne Rylon

Editing by Mackenzie Walton

Proofreading by Fedora Chen

Formatting by Jayne Rylon

ABOUT THE BOOK

The original Powertools crew is back in a brand new series!

Starting over is never easy. Especially when it means leaving your friends and lovers behind.

An accident on the Hot Rods construction site draws Mike to Middletown. Not to assume his role as foreman, but to help his best friend, Joe, learn the ropes. It's his turn to be caught off balance when his wife delivers shocking news.

The rest of the Powertools crew join them to attend a wedding at their friends' motorcycle garage, Hot Rides. The night could change everything—both personally and professionally.

Because while celebrating their friends' new commitment, it's nearly impossible to deny the strength of their own complicated bonds or the fact that they're evolving. Their marriages, their friendships, and their futures hang in the balance.

At the end of the festivities, who will stay and who will go?

ADDITIONAL INFORMATION

Sign up for the Naughty News for contests, release updates, news, appearance information, sneak peek excerpts, reading-themed apparel deals, and more. www.jaynerylon.com/newsletter

Shop for autographed books, reading-themed apparel, goodies, and more www.jaynerylon.com/shop

A complete list of Jayne's books can be found at www.jaynerylon.com/books

1

I t happened in slow motion.

Joe barely kept his temper during a phone argument he was having with a supplier over a messed up delivery. Part of his team stood by on hold. They'd been interrupted by the phone ringing while revising their plans due to yet another issue that had cropped up that morning. As Joe glanced away, praying for sanity in the midst of the chaos that came with managing the construction of the Hot Rods' home extension, he saw it about to happen.

One of the new guys framing the roof picked up a pneumatic nail gun and yanked on the air hose. Right about the same time as one of the other workers—it looked like Adam from where Joe was standing—attempted to straddle a larger than usual gap between two studs with a truss balanced on his shoulder. Instead of planting on lumber, Adam's boot got tangled in the whipping hose that snaked across his path at precisely the wrong moment.

It was something that never would have happened in

the Powertools crew. Joe and the guys, and Devon, knew each other in and out. They worked seamlessly together, like a well-choreographed dance troupe. Each of them moved in time with the others whether they were working on a construction project or screwing around together. Literally.

Sleeping with your partners gave your work relationship a whole new sort of intimacy, he supposed. The crew were always aware of each other and fit together seamlessly, which he realized right about then he might have taken for granted after nearly two decades of friendship. He was an idiot for leaving. For thinking he could recreate that overnight and handle being in charge —especially of a job of this scale.

"Look out!" another one of the young guys Joe had hired to work on this special project, away from his regular crew, shouted the warning but it was too late.

First Adam jerked, then he lost control of the load on his shoulder. A timber rained onto the ground floor of the site. Each inch it travelled downward took ten beats of Joe's racing heart. It clipped one of the other crewmen, who was at least wearing his hard hat, before clattering to the cement slab that made the foundation of the building they were erecting. Unfortunately, Adam's wind-milling arms couldn't keep him in place.

Joe lunged forward as if he could reach the guy and snatch him from midair although he was watching the horrific scene unfold from at least fifty feet away. And when Adam crashed into the ground, landing shin-first on top of the wood he'd dropped, everyone on the site let out a collective groan in response to the sickening crunch.

Already in motion, Joe disconnected his call but kept

his phone in his hand as he sprinted toward the injured man.

"Ah, fuck." Adam rolled, clutching his leg. "Fuck!"

Joe was relieved that the lucky bastard was able to curse at all. He could easily have broken his neck or damaged his spine or punctured a lung with a broken rib. Any number of other things. Hell, he still might have even though he could shout.

Joe slid across the remaining ground between them as if he were stealing home at the Powertools annual cutthroat summer barbeque softball game. He put a hand on Adam's shoulder and held him in place gently yet as firmly as he could. He kept the other man from rocking or trying to get to his feet out of sheer instinct.

"Hey. You're gonna be okay. Stay still until we can get someone out here to check you out. Just a few minutes, I promise."

The rest of the guys circled around, watching as Joe dialed 911 and relayed information about the accident and their location to the emergency operator as quickly and efficiently as possible. He hovered over the wounded worker, inspecting him for signs of visible trauma. Blood trickled from his fattening lip. Adam's eyes started to dilate and glaze with pain.

It reminded Joe of those times when Dave had been recovering in the hospital after his accident, many years in the past. He'd never forget this same cold feeling of dread taking up residence in his gut. And just like he had done then, he put on his bravest face and lied through his clenched teeth.

"You're okay, Adam. You're good. Help is coming. Everything's going to be fine."

About that time, a booming voice shouted, "Hey, cuz, what's going on?"

Eli.

Shit!

Not only had Joe allowed one of his crew to get hurt, now his cousin and one of the men he respected most in the world was going to witness his epic failure. He wouldn't blame Eli if he changed his mind and hired a new foreman to build his home. It was becoming more and more apparent that Joe was way out of his league. This was Eli's future house, the place he would bring his baby to in a few months. He'd want it to be perfect, not haunted by the ghosts of construction accidents or full of flaws caused by his family's poor management abilities.

Eli parted the ring of shocked workers and crouched down on Adam's other side, without looking in the least ruffled. He took one look at Joe's face, which was probably whiter than spray foam insulation fresh from the can, and said, "Ambulance on the way?"

Joe nodded, unable to speak.

Eli squeezed Adam's shoulder gently, then stood, already off to assist. That's what a true leader did, while Joe felt frozen inside. "I'll meet the paramedics out by the street and bring them back. Hang in there, buddy."

Things started happening really fast then, making up for the time warp that had stretched the instants it took Adam to drop from the sky. Soon people were crawling all over the spot like ants on a piece of hard candy. Paramedics, cops, Uncle Tom and Ms. Brown, the rest of the Hot Rods... Hell, the star of Hollywood's latest blockbuster might have been there too, but Joe wouldn't have noticed.

He stuck by Adam's side until they loaded him in the

ambulance and would have ridden along except the guy who'd yanked the hose came up beside him then. "Mind if I go instead? It's my fault. I…I'm so sorry. I totally understand if you fire me. I can't believe I did this. Adam… hurt…because of my dumb ass."

Joe didn't respond, unsure of what the hell the right protocol was in this situation. Mike or even Eli would have known what to say. He had no clue how to strike the balance between stern reprimand and reassurance.

As he debated, Adam shrugged one shoulder and said, "I know you didn't do it on purpose. Yeah, Cole, I'd appreciate it if you'd come along. If that's all right with the boss. And, Joe, please don't can him. It wasn't only his mistake. I should have been paying better attention."

Joe looked between the two, his eyes narrowing as he caught a spark of something awfully familiar between them. He'd fucked up a bunch already, but he didn't want to interfere with whatever was happening there on a personal level. "Yeah, of course. It's Adam's call. I'll drive over to see how you're doing as soon as they're done with me here."

Adam winced as he shifted on the gurney. Cole was there, adjusting his pillow before saying something Joe couldn't make out. The ambulance squad settled into place, too. Just before the driver shut the back doors, Adam called, "Thanks, foreman."

"For what?" Joe nearly fell on his ass.

"For keeping me calm. And getting help so fast." He let his head fall back then. "And for doing the right thing with Cole. Thanks for giving a shit."

Eli came up behind Joe and put his hand on his cousin's back as the doors were closed and the vehicle's sirens drowned out any chance Joe had at formulating some kind of response.

After the flashing red lights disappeared around a bend in the wooded forest road and the siren had faded to a dreadful wail, Eli asked, "You okay?"

"Me? *I* didn't just take a header off the fucking roof." Joe punched his palm. "I should never have let them be doing both of those tasks at the same time."

"Did you tell them to?" Eli wondered.

"No. But I wasn't paying enough attention. I didn't see it until it was too late. What the hell am I doing here?" Joe looked to Eli, tugging the hair his fingers were now tangled in.

"Hey, calm down. This is what you have insurance for." Eli squeezed Joe's shoulder. "Accidents happen. Construction is dangerous work."

When Joe still didn't say anything, Eli lowered his voice and asked, "You *do* have insurance, right?"

"Yeah. Yeah, of course. But we've never had to use it before at Powertools. And here I am having to dig out the policy already." Joe swallowed hard. It was the foreman's responsibility to look out for the crew, and he'd failed. Big time. It was only his second week on the damn job and he'd already shown that he wasn't cut out for it.

And that was even before he factored in the supplier drama, and the issues implementing the designs they'd drafted. What the hell had he been thinking when he'd told Eli he'd do this and moved his entire family several states away from everything they'd ever known on the hope that he could pull this off?

"Hey. That guy is going to be fine." Eli lowered his voice as he came around to Joe's front and braced his hands on Joe's shoulders before shaking him a little bit.

"You can beat yourself up later. Get out there, talk to your crew. Reassure them and then think about what could have prevented this. Make some new policies and ensure the guys follow them from now on. This is how you get better."

"Yeah. Yeah. That sounds good." Joe nodded. Why hadn't he thought of a plan like that? Probably because he was just a worker bee who'd never intended to be the one in charge.

That was Mike's job, and he was doing a piss-poor imitation of it.

One thought reverberated in Joe's mind. The one that he'd drilled into his head by repeating it constantly as the responsibility he'd taken on for his cousin Eli began to overwhelm him.

You're not a foreman. You were never meant to do this. You're not good at it and someone's going to get hurt...again... maybe worse next time because of you. There's still time to bail. To go home.

"Whatever you do, don't let them see you freaking out," Eli cautioned. "When you're done, come to my office. And we'll do that together. Then I'll drive you over to the hospital, okay?"

Was this what Mike did? Did he vent to Kate or pace his office alone at night when the burden of being in charge got too heavy? Joe felt like a bastard because he'd never even considered that possibility when he went home to his family and slept like a baby.

Even now, Eli was teaching him how to remain in control, because he didn't have the faintest clue about how to be the example Mike had always been for them.

"Okay, right." Joe swiped his hand over his mouth and tried his best to get it together. The men milling aimlessly around the job site deserved that much from him at least.

"You got this." Eli watched him go.

So Joe straightened his back and channeled Mike, thinking of what he was going to say to his crew. And then how he'd admit his fuck-up to his own foreman later that night.

2

Mike kicked off his boots, then walked through his kitchen to kiss Kate, who was helping Abby and Landry with their homework. His wife was pretty much a superhero, juggling her own interior design and antique restoration business along with managing their family.

"Want me to cook dinner?" he asked as he ruffled his son's hair and gave his daughter a quick one-armed hug before she could object. Teenagers. *Ugh.*

"Can we order food instead?" Landry asked, looking up from his math workbook with such a hopeful look that all Mike could do was laugh.

"Yeah. I mean, I'd vote for pizza over my lame attempt at grilling any day too."

"You make great barbecue chicken thighs," Kate looked up, then winced. "But I'm not very hungry, so maybe takeout isn't a bad idea."

She avoided Mike's stare when he looked over to scan her as if he could see any illness zooming in the air around her head like neon-green cartoon germs. Too many times lately, Kate had begged off dinner and even his offer of breakfast in bed last weekend. Was she sick? Or was what he had offered her that much worse than she was used to since Joe wasn't around to cook for both their families? The other guy had often made himself at home in their kitchen or on the grill when he and Morgan and their kids would swing by to spend the evening together with Mike and his family.

Except Mike's best friend had ditched them and moved a few states over to Middletown in order to be closer to his family, especially his cousin Eli. The Hot Rods garage owner was expecting a child and needed some help expanding their living quarters beyond the second story over their business.

"Everyone good with pepperoni?" Mike asked as he brought up a food delivery app on his phone.

"Yeah!" Landry fist pumped and even Abby nodded with a small smirk. He'd take that. She'd been out of sorts since Joe's son Nathan had left for the summer. The two of them were maybe even closer than Mike and Joe or Morgan and Kate, who'd been best friends since elementary school.

For a blissful hour or so everything was fine. Normal. Happy.

"This was a good idea, kid." Mike gave Landry credit where it was due as he polished off another slice of pizza.

They were laughing as Abby ignored them and focused on her phone instead. Kate shot him a warning glance, but Mike shook his head no, subtly. Hell, their daughter was probably texting Nathan. So he left her alone. One meal in peace was worth a hell of a lot to him these days.

"Dad?" Abby asked around a mouth full of gooey cheese, surprising him.

"Yeah?" He looked up and the last bit of crust became awfully hard to swallow. Fine lines creased the perfect, smooth skin between her eyebrows. They were even more pronounced than they would have been otherwise since she'd recently become obsessed with watching videos online about shaping and makeup and all sorts of things he wasn't ready to deal with in regards to his baby girl just yet. Kate permitted her to test out stuff in the house, but it was still a shock to see her looking so damn grown up. And now, worried. "What's wrong?"

"You better call Uncle Joe. Nathan said something bad happened and everyone is freaking out."

"*Bad*? What kind of bad?" Kate stood up straight and then turned a bit ashen before sinking back into her chair.

Damn it. Everything was falling apart.

"An accident." Landry was looking at the hand-me-down phone he'd talked Mike into activating so he could stay in touch with Klea and Nathan now that Joe's kids were out of their area code. "Somebody got hurt. Not Uncle Joe. Somebody who works for him."

"Shit!" Mike stood from the table, his chair scraping on the floor as he jammed his hand into his pocket. But just as he touched his own phone, it began to buzz beneath his fingers. He hauled it out and went onto the patio to talk in case he had to shield the kids from something gruesome. Hopefully Nathan wouldn't text them pictures before he could find out if everyone was okay. Physically and beyond.

Bad shit could go down on a construction site. They'd been lucky to avoid anything serious at Powertools the past twenty years, but that didn't mean it couldn't happen to anyone at any time.

And Joe was new to this...

It was a lot of responsibility to be the one shouldering that burden. Mike knew that all too well. Maybe he could lend some support, even from far away.

"What happened?" Mike barked as he connected the call from Joe.

"I should have been paying more attention. I didn't see they were working close enough to get crossed up. The roofing framers, I mean. Adam got tangled in Cole's pneumatic hose and fell from the second story while carrying some trusses. Looks like he fractured his tibia and maybe screwed up his kneecap too. I watched him fall like some shit out of *The Matrix*, except I couldn't get there in time. But fuck, it could have been worse. So much worse. And it would have been my fault."

"No, it wouldn't have been. That's not your job."

"To take on everyone's issues? Accept blame for whatever happens? Could have fooled me. The buck stops with the foreman, doesn't it? At least it does when you're the one running things. I don't know that I'm cut out to be one of those. I'm not you." Joe sounded miserable.

Was that what he did? Mike wasn't sure. He did his best for the guys, and the woman, in his crew. Not to mention the rest of their lovers and kids when they were outside of work. But right now he couldn't do shit to protect Joe or help him carry the burden he knew was heavy as fuck. As much as he wished he could take charge and solve the problem or, hell, even just hug the guy...

His arms weren't long enough to reach.

"If I could do this for you, I would." Mike pinched the bridge of his nose.

"You can't. I signed up for this, and if I don't follow through I'm going to let Eli and Uncle Tom and the rest of the Hot Rods down. On the other hand, if I don't know what the fuck I'm doing, someone could literally die—" Joe cut off with a strangled groan that made Mike sure he'd thought that was a possibility earlier in the day.

"Look. Maybe I can come out there for the weekend. Go over your plans and help you do a safety review with everyone. Would that help?"

"I don't know if it would improve my skills magically, but it would make me feel better. To know I'm not missing something simple that's going to get one of these guys maimed at least." Joe sighed. "Are you sure?"

"Yeah, of course. I want to come. We were all heading that way in a week anyway for Kyra, Ollie, and Van's party. Maybe I'll just stay. Let me talk to Kate about it and make sure she's okay by herself with the kids for a few days and then I'll call you right back."

"See. Even now you're covering my ass." Joe shook his head, but the glimmer of relief in his tone was reward enough.

"I do enjoy doing that from time to time." Mike figured if dirty jokes didn't make Joe loosen up, nothing would.

Fortunately, his friend gave a halfhearted chuckle. "Come out here, save it, and you can do whatever you want with it. Deal?"

"You know I'd do this no matter what. Just because you fucking left us doesn't mean I don't care anymore." Mike hadn't meant to sound so bitter, but maybe part of him had been stung and even a tad jealous. The Hot Rods project was a big deal. Hell, with their reality show, it would probably land Joe a million new jobs that could keep him in Middletown for the next decade instead of only the summer. For a split second, Mike wondered if he should convince Joe to come home instead of helping, but no, that was selfish and he was a dick to even think it.

Joe groaned. "I'm an idiot, I know. Thanks for standing by me anyway, Mike."

"Always. I'll call you in a little bit. Go check on your crewman, and try to cut yourself a break."

"I will if next time you have some problem like this, you lean on me too. You shouldn't have to shoulder this shit by yourself. I'm sorry I was too ignorant to realize you've been doing it all this time. Or to take advantage of handing the stress off to you. Your job sucks, you know that?"

"Only sometimes." Mike felt something in his chest ease. "But I'll take you up on that. Thanks. Talk to you soon."

3

---

ike was glad to see the kids had gone to their rooms when he wandered back into the kitchen. Kate, however, was cleaning with a ferociousness that could only mean she was trying to alleviate some of her tension. He could think of better ways to do that for her.

He crossed to her, took the washcloth from her hand, and set it aside before gathering her into his arms. She smelled like sunshine and summer, just like she had the first day he'd rescued her from falling off a roof. Not so different from what Joe had wanted to do for his crewman earlier.

"It's going to be okay." Mike hugged her.

"Promise?"

"Yeah. A worker fell from the second story."

"Shit." Kate looked up at him with wide, worried eyes. The fear of heights had never quite left her after her near miss.

"He'll be all right. Busted his leg but got off pretty lucky, to be honest."

"What about Joe?" she asked, still not relieved. The bond between the Powertools crew ran deeper than the professional connection between the construction workers. They were a unit, had been for damn near twenty years now.

"His ego might be more shattered than that other guy's leg." Mike stroked his fingers through her hair until she melted against him. "Would it be okay with you if I went out there this weekend? Maybe for a few days, or even until you guys come out for the wedding stuff? To double check him on his plans and his procedures so he feels more comfortable?"

Kate hesitated, which actually surprised him. She was always the first to offer to help someone out. Of course, he hadn't forgotten about her acting a bit weird earlier either.

"If not, that's okay. I'll figure out another way." Mike started imagining how they might do things over video conference and screen share, although he understood that Joe needed someone to hold his hand more than he needed any of that other shit. He was a solid construction worker and had decades of experience.

It was only his confidence that needed bolstering.

"No, no. It's fine." Kate patted his chest. "We'll be good for a week. You're right. It doesn't make sense for you to go and come back just to turn around and head out there again."

"If Landry and Abby didn't have swim camp, I'd take the kids with me." Mike thought of how he might lighten Kate's burden too. Maybe Joe was right. He did it automatically, all the time, and sometimes it could be exhausting. But he wouldn't change it for the world.

"You're so sweet." Kate leaned into him, tipping her face up. And he wasn't about to ignore the offer. "But no, they're fine. We'll do okay without you even if we'll miss you every single minute."

Mike smiled. They didn't need him, but it was nice to know they liked having him around anyway. He lowered his head and brushed his lips against Kate's, loving how even now she could fire him up despite the tense circumstances.

Or maybe because of them.

Kate was his relief. She was the one who talked him down and helped him work out his worries and frustrations in a much more productive way than ruminating on them. "You know you saved me, right?"

She paused and angled her head as she stared into his eyes. "How so?"

"I might have caught you that day on the roof, but every day since you've made my life easier, you've kept me happy, and you brought the crew together not just for a good time now and then, but for life. It's you, Kate. You're our glue."

"Of everyone, I fell for you because you take care of them so well." Kate caressed his cheek. "You never understood how special it is that you can be a leader and still one of them. It's not nothing. I love you for it."

Mike shrugged. "It's just what I do."

"I know, and that's why it's sexy as hell."

"You think so?" He grinned at his wife.

"I do." She beamed right back.

Without thinking, he slid his hand beneath the hem of her skirt and lifted it, exposing her stomach. Suddenly, he was ready for dessert. Making love to her would never get old. Neither would it get boring despite the adventures they shared with the rest of the crew.

Kate could blow his mind without even trying, and fortunately she liked doing it often.

"Mike...the kids..."

"Need to learn to stay out of the kitchen when I'm hungry."

She laughed, but she lost concentration on the feeling of him stroking her soft skin and instead kept peeking over her shoulder nervously.

"Come on." Mike took her hand and led her out the side door onto the patio. Lush green plants, most of them part of her edible herb garden, and flowers that blossomed in a riot of colors screened them from the view of the neighbors and from most of the windows of their house.

He trapped her against the brick wall. It must have warmed her back, infusing her tense muscles with heat that helped to relax them almost as much as the caresses and kisses he began to lavish on her.

"The kids..." she objected again, this time less vehemently.

"Aren't gonna bother looking for us when they're talking to Klea and Nathan." Mike saw she wasn't entirely buying his logic, so he spun around and grabbed the grill, wheeling it in front of the door. The massive six-burner loaded down with a full gas tank and the essential tools that went with it ensured the door couldn't open even an inch. "Better?"

Kate laughed. "Yeah. That'll hold them for a few minutes. Enough to get dressed if necessary. But don't start something if you're not sure you can stand being interrupted."

"In that case, I guess I'd better hurry." Mike leaned in again, this time dipping his head to rake his teeth along her neck. And where she'd seemed tired and kind of queasy not too long ago, he did his best to chase those sensations away and replace them with pure fire.

"Yes, you should do that." Kate reached for his jeans and unbuttoned them with a practiced flick of her fingers that still riled him every time she did it.

He lifted her into his arms and her legs wrapped, automatically, around his hips as they had so often before.

"Are you sure your back is up to this?" she asked, entirely serious.

"It could be broken and I'd figure something out." He tugged her closer. "But I'm not lying. It's been feeling better than it has in years since I got that epidural steroid shot a couple weeks ago."

If she doubted him for an instant, she wouldn't let him hurt himself, no matter how good it felt to her. Kate was more like him than she knew. Getting old sucked, but he wasn't ready to allow any aches or pains to keep him from what they were about to do. He wasn't dead yet.

"Well, if it's sore I'll rub it later," she promised. "How's that?"

"You can rub it even if it's not," he said with a smirk that caused her to laugh again and smack his shoulder. Hearing it made him even harder than he had been when she'd opened his jeans. Making Kate happy was his favorite pastime.

Even more, Kate understood that he needed this as much as she did. It killed him to feel so out of control when it came to Joe and the crew. Being separated lately was bad enough, but being far away when his best friend needed him...well, that wasn't a feeling he was comfortable with.

As his desire to be in charge grew, she let him take control.

Mike growled as she turned pliant in his arms. He flashed her a wolfish smile before kissing the shit out of her. As he did, he rocked against her, impressing on her how hard he was and how well he was about to fuck her with arcs of his hips that stroked his hard cock over her mound.

Glad that she'd worn a simple sundress that day in an attempt to avoid the amplified effects the heat seemed to have on her lately, Mike hiked one of Kate's thighs onto his hip, letting the silky fabric fall away.

He reached beneath it to her panties and yanked, ripping them from her in a move he'd perfected over the years. Thank god she enjoyed shopping for pretty new lingerie.

The lace fluttered downward and draped over one of the plants.

Suddenly Kate's need became ferocious and his matched her mounting desire. Fortunately, she'd always been able to do that for him, ramp him up. Even if that meant cheering him on as he orchestrated the crew's group-sex sessions.

She reached between them and yanked his jeans open wide, making him grateful the zipper didn't maul his dick given the fact that he hadn't bothered with underwear that day...or most.

Too bad the Powertools were scattered right now, focused on a number of different projects and stretched out across several states. Otherwise he might have called an emergency gathering.

Until they could be together again next weekend, Kate would be more than enough.

His hands gravitated to her ass, holding her at the exact right level for him to increase the pressure of his hard-on stroking against her. He adjusted his stance, angling his hips so that the next time they ground together, the blunt tip nudged her opening instead of gliding past it.

Kate cracked him up when she adjusted her dress, shielding the spot where they joined from view. Too bad. He'd never get tired of watching them come together and his flesh fuse with hers.

On the brink of penetrating, he paused.

"You're not teasing me, are you?" Kate glared.

She nipped his lower lip, making him chuckle. "Never. You want it?"

The desperate sound she made would have probably embarrassed her with anyone but Mike or the rest of the crew. After decades together, she trusted them completely even with the most vulnerable parts of her psyche. The facets of herself she revealed only to them.

So he figured he should reward her for her candor.

"It's yours," Mike said without waiting for her response. He groaned as he rocked forward, lodging a few inches within her. It shocked and thrilled him that she could still make him feel this good, that his body fit hers so perfectly. It was exciting every time.

Kate threw her head back, rapping it on the wall, as she tried to worm her way down his shaft. Mike held her hips in his steely grip and ignored the pleading of her body as he filled her at his own steady, relentless pace. He kissed her so that she had to lean forward a bit and wouldn't hurt herself again.

Deeper and deeper he slid into her, working her open,

as she did her best not to scream her satisfaction and blow what little cover they had.

Even years of practice didn't take away the thrill of burying himself within her fully. Mike filled her completely, possessed her from the inside out. And she loved every second, raking his back with her neat, short nails.

When he was balls-deep in her, he paused, brushing the hair from her face so he could crush his mouth to hers. This kiss was different than the others. Urgent and possessive. Mike's tongue swept into her mouth, parrying with hers as she met him swipe for swipe.

Her fingers dug into his shoulders as she tried to show him what she needed: for him to move.

So he did.

Mike retreated a bit, making her whimper, but only until he drilled into her. He took her fast and hard against the wall, refusing to go easy when she'd told him often that it made her proud to know she could handle all of him, in and out of bed...or against a wall. She spread her legs, sure he wouldn't let her fall as his hips hammered hers. And she was right about that. He wouldn't drop her now or ever.

However, this wasn't going to be one of their legendary all-night fuckathons. It was going to be fast, hard, raw, and so damn powerful they didn't need hours to be satisfied.

When his chest mashed to hers, she gasped. "What the hell did you just do to me?"

"This?" He rubbed against her, repeating the motion. Sensitive in a way she wasn't always when it came to her breasts, she clamped down on his dick at the contact.

"Fuck yeah, Kate," he rumbled against her neck, just below her ear. "You needed this too, didn't you?"

"Yes," she gasped. "And I didn't even realize how bad until right now."

Things were odd lately, off balance since Joe and Morgan had left the group. None of them wanted to admit it, but they all knew it was likely to be more than a seasonal change. They'd lost an integral part of their crew, and the rough, furious fucking Mike was giving his wife was filling part of the void with overwhelming passion.

He was a man of action, but lately there hadn't been anything he could to do to fix the crew's problems. This at least he could take care of for them both.

He pumped into her with long, steady glides that had her biting her lip, presumably to keep from screaming for more. She didn't have to anyway, because no way in hell was he stopping before they'd taken each other over the edge.

Kate arched her back, her eyes slamming shut when his torso tapped her clit as he bottomed out in her again and again.

"There? Right there?" he asked, though he already knew the effect he had on her. He couldn't have missed it when her pussy began to tighten around him, hugging his cock so hard it made it more difficult for him to thrust into her.

Of course, that seemed to spiral Kate's pleasure higher as he stroked over her tensed muscles.

"Mike," she whisper-shouted, clutching him tighter to her. "Damn."

His muscles bunched beneath her hands. He worked hard all day and it showed. At least he had that going for him.

"If you go, you're going to take me with you. Sorry, I

can't hold out. Not today. Not like this." He groaned and shuddered as he plunged into her once more.

"Better come with me," she grumbled.

He understood what she didn't have the capacity to say right then. It wouldn't be fair if she was the only one about to lose her mind from his skilled fucking. She liked him to be equally as devastated as she was when she let go like this.

He smiled at her and redoubled his efforts.

Mike leaned against her, trapping her between the rough wall and his taut body. His ass clenched beneath her heels as he rode her, intent on bringing them both as much bliss as possible. And when he added a little grind at the peak of each stroke, being sure to rub her clit as he pressed his dick against the most sensitive place inside her, he knew coming was inevitable for them both.

She tried to warn him she was going to tip, but he shushed her, encouraging her to let go.

So she did. Kate flew apart in his arms, proving again that she was certain he'd support her as she lost herself in the ecstasy he gave her. The thing that never ceased to amaze him was that her pleasure alone was enough to set him off too—the clamping of her pussy around his cock triggered his orgasm.

He bit her shoulder and grunted as he began to flood her, the motions of her involuntary spasms milking him dry. She stared up at the sky, gasping for air to fill her lungs while rapture wrung her entire being.

Her toes curled and her fingers clenched. Then all at once, she relaxed.

Mike nuzzled the crook of her neck as he too began to recover, smooshing them together from collarbones to hips. "Damn, Kate. I needed that. I needed you."

She ran her fingers through his hair, when it was still too difficult to speak much.

His chest heaved against her as he sucked in a full breath of air, maybe for the first time since Abby had told them there had been an accident.

Though Mike had been supportive of Joe and his move out to Middletown, it wasn't easy for him. Or for any of the crew. Especially not when the way they dealt with turbulent times had always involved coming together as a group for a physical release as epic, or even more so, than the one he and Kate had just shared.

"You always know where to find me when you need me," she murmured before kissing him gently. "I promise I'll always to be here like you've always been for me. For all of the crew."

Mike slipped from her and tucked himself away before straightening her dress. They were still kissing, floating down together, when a loud smack from the direction of the kitchen made them both jump.

"Dad?" The door banged into the grill a second time.

Kate raised a brow, then whispered to Mike. "See?"

Mike only laughed. "We were done."

She scrubbed her face with her hands as if she could wipe away any traces of the passion they'd shared and leave only happy satisfaction in its place. After verifying her clothes and his own were in order, Mike scooted the grill away from the door enough that Landry could squeeze through the gap.

"What's up?" Mike asked.

"Klea said Uncle Joe is better now." Landry reported.

Whether it was the positive news or the way he'd vented his pent-up tension, Mike flashed an honest, relaxed smile. The kind his family expected from him most of the time. "That's good. Real good."

"Did you tell him accidents happen? Like that time I hit the baseball through the windshield of Mom's car and thought you were going to ground me for a million years?"

"I did, yeah." Mike ruffled Landry's hair. He was always impressed by the things his son learned from him even without being directly taught. The way he looked after everyone around him was eerily familiar, too. He was going to be a hell of a man one day.

Landry peered beyond them then, squinting at the flash of white in the flower bush. "What's that?"

Fortunately Kate was faster than him. She lunged for her destroyed underwear, snatched them up, and tucked them into her pocket before their son could get a better look. Thank God it hadn't been Abby, because she had a better bullshit meter than her brother, even though she was barely a teenager.

"Just a rag." Kate shrugged casually with one shoulder, her fist still planted in her pocket, obscuring the evidence. "I was cleaning up a few things out here. Let Dad put the grill away and we can go inside. I think there's still a few slices left if you need an after-dinner snack."

"Oh yeah!" Landry had already spun around and wandered toward the pizza boxes for a second round. The kid was starting to eat anything and everything in the house.

Sure enough, Abby was inside leaning against the fridge, her arms crossed. When she took in Mike giving Kate one last lingering kiss full of promise to take his time much, much later, the girl shook her head. "You two are so gross."

Good thing she didn't yet realize they did more than make out and cuddle on the couch during movie nights.

"Yup. And you just keep right on thinking boys are icky. Until you're sixty at least. I'm fine with that." Mike cracked open a beer and downed at least a third in a few huge gulps before asking Landry to hand him a slice of the now-cold pizza.

He smiled when even Kate nibbled at a piece, obviously having worked up a bit of an appetite.

4

Kate tried not to let it bother her that Mike was getting farther and farther from her as each moment passed. But they'd been together for so many years now that it felt like part of her was missing when he wasn't there. Something important. Like her heart.

She pressed her hand to her middle, annoyed by the tears that sprang to her eyes even as her stomach knotted. It wasn't like her to be this needy, and it kind of pissed her off. Her emotions were all over the place. What. The. Fuck.

Before she could dwell on it, she heard a rap at the back door. Only a few people used that entrance to their house, and the call that followed made it clear which one of them it was. "Hey, Kate. Open up. I need to look for something in Mike's office."

Devon. The lone woman on the Powertools construction crew. She knew a thing or two about being tough.

Kate swallowed the acid that was clawing at her throat and rushed to fling open the gorgeous custom doors the crew had built to let in more light and add yet another special touch to the home they'd created together.

"Sorry, can't chat." Devon gave Kate an air kiss as she squeezed past and headed down the hall to Mike's office as if she lived there. Hell, she'd spent enough time in their house over the years for that to nearly be true, and in the crew everyone was at home in each other's spaces. But this was a bit much even for Devon, who was more like one of the guys than a member of the wives' club.

"What's going on?" Kate trailed behind the petite woman, who made up for her lack of stature with a huge personality and nearly unshakable confidence. "Can I help?"

"Uh, maybe?" Devon plopped into Mike's seat and flipped open his laptop. "You know the password to this thing?"

"Probably something with the kids' names." Kate shrugged.

"Nah. It'll be yours." Devon looked up at her with an incredulous stare. "How could you not realize that?"

And when Devon did, she hesitated, her eyes narrowing a bit.

"What?" Kate asked.

"You okay?"

"Yeah. I mean, I think so. It's just been stressful lately, you know? Tell me what's wrong with you." Kate couldn't handle much more. She already felt off kilter and had been fighting exhaustion for weeks.

"I need the contract for the spray foam insulation guys." Devon swiped her hand over her face before pecking out a password attempt on Mike's laptop and hitting enter. Nope. Not that one. "We waited all fucking morning for them and they never showed. They're blaming the screw up on Mike when they clearly lost our appointment. They're holding up our timeline. We can't start putting the place back together until they're done, and now they're saying it's going to take another three weeks to get back on the schedule."

"Weren't you already on the verge of being late to deliver the house since you're down a man with Joe gone?" Kate groaned. Mike prided himself on doing what he promised their clients. He would not be happy about this. But he could only do so much, and be in so many places, at once.

"Yup." Devon grimaced and then tried another password. Her curse made it clear she'd failed. Of course they could call Mike, and maybe they'd have to in the end, but Kate didn't want to bug her husband any more than Devon or the rest of the crew obviously cared to either.

"Humor me. Try the kids' names." Kate leaned in.

"I did. That was the second one. I'm telling you..." Devon pecked out something else and tapped enter. The computer's lock screen disappeared. "Bingo!"

"His password was *bingo*?"

"No...it's ILoveKate69."

"Shut up. It is not." Kate rolled her eyes.

"Totally is." Devon laughed. "Try it yourself. He's such a pussy. And extremely predictable."

"Don't let him hear you say that or he'll devise some plan to make you beg next time the crew is playing together." Kate arched a brow, though her insides were melting from how sweet her husband could be. Lately things had been tense, but maybe if he could help Joe and she could keep the crew on track while he was away…

Maybe things could get back to something like normal. Then maybe this anxiety or whatever it was causing her to feel so out of sorts would ease up too.

"Still not finding a reason not to push him." Devon winked.

Kate shook her head. "Maybe that's what we all need. Some time to blow off steam together. Thank God we have the trip to Middletown next weekend and plenty of babysitters out there too."

Devon studied Kate again. To distract her friend from finding anything too concerning she might then blab to Mike about, Kate pointed to his laptop. "He keeps all his contracts in a folder on the cloud drive."

Devon swung around, her focus on hunting down the paperwork they both knew would be there. Mike didn't mess up shit like that. He ran his construction jobs with military precision. If he said the insulators should have been there, she had no doubt they were supposed to have shown.

"Got it!" Devon leaned in, then cursed. "See! Those assholes think they can weasel out of this just because Mike isn't there to shove his steel-toed boot up their ass. Little do they know that I'm twice as mean as he is."

"And I'm even worse." Kate snatched up her phone and said, "Read me their number. I'll call for you. Unless you want the honors…"

"Honestly, nah." Devon gave her the digits. "I'm better at knocking sense into things with my tools than talking about it. Do you mind?"

Kate shook her head. After a few minutes of explaining the situation and getting the same bullshit response Devon had earlier, she dug deep and applied her best mom-intimidation. "I have a contract right here that says otherwise. If you're no longer able to abide by the terms, then we'll expect a fifty-percent discount in order to offer our client compensation for the delay in delivery your mistake is going to cause. Their house has already sold, so they will need to be put up in a hotel and alter their move-in plans, all of which will make this mistake very costly."

"Ma'am, where's Mike?" Oh, she bet they were wishing for her husband now. He relied on charm and his good nature to persuade people where she believed in being much more direct.

"He's busy. Powertools has given you plenty of business throughout the years. This is not a time to let us down. You know we have contacts in every area of this industry and we won't hesitate to let our peers know that you're no longer reliable and that you're dishonest as well."

Devon mouthed, *Yeah, tell them!*

"Uh, that's...unnecessary," the contractor practically squeaked.

"Then you'll be at the site tomorrow to complete the work as indicated in our contract?"

"We'll have to start at the ass crack of dawn so we can squeeze in two jobs."

"So long as you are at our property first, our crew will meet you any time you like to oversee the installation." Kate peeked over at Devon, who was nodding enthusiastically and flashing a thumbs-up.

A sigh loud enough that Devon had to be able to hear it rattled her ear. "I guess we'll see you at four o'clock then. Or will Mike be back?"

Devon snorted when she heard the wishful note in the guy's voice.

"He's out of town working on another project. Devon will be the one in charge. Talk to her about anything you need and make sure the work is completed to her satisfaction."

"Yes, ma'am."

"Thank you," Kate said sweetly before hanging up with a flourish and jab of her index finger.

"Holy shit!" Devon crossed the gap between them and squeezed her. Despite being petite, she was strong as shit from working construction and lifted Kate like she hadn't put on an extra few pounds or ten lately. Then she started to swing her around. "You're so good at that! Why doesn't Mike have you do that for us all the time? Usually he just curses a bunch and promises to buy beer when they're finished."

"Really?" Kate laughed because she could totally picture it. Until Devon made one more revolution and her stomach lurched. "Uhhh, stop. Please."

Devon kept cracking up and didn't take her quite as seriously as she should have. Kate shoved at her friend's shoulders until they broke apart and she stumbled away, staggering toward the hall bathroom.

She braced her hands on cool counter top, slammed her eyes closed, and focused on taking long, deep breaths until the world stopped glitching around her.

Devon was there, rubbing her back, encouraging her quietly. "Hey, you're okay. You're okay. Sorry, I didn't mean to fuck you up."

"It's not you." Kate moaned as her queasiness passed. She splashed her face with cold water, then carefully turned and sank onto the closed toilet, folding until her head rested on her stacked arms.

"Then what the hell is it?" Devon wondered.

"I don't know. Stress? I haven't felt right for weeks." Kate groaned.

"Weeks? And what kind of *not right*?" Devon crouched down and scanned Kate's pale face and the gaunt bags she knew were darkening the skin beneath her eyes lately.

"I feel like shit."

"Obviously." Devon tipped her head. "How have you been hiding this from Mike, and why?"

"He's got enough on his plate." Kate sighed. "He's been preoccupied with Joe and keeping the rest of you from getting as upset as I think he is."

"Okay, fine. So tell me then." Devon squeezed her knee. "What's bugging you?"

"I'm run down. Tired all the time. I'm starving, but every time I get near food it turns my stomach. I just about climbed Mike outside on the patio last night and I would have gone for about ten more rounds, but I fell asleep the instant my head hit the pillow. I'm cranky and anxious and..."

"Holy shit. When the hell are you going to learn?" Devon flung open the cabinet under the sink. When she apparently didn't find what she was after, she popped to her feet to rummage through the medicine cabinet too.

"What are you looking for?"

"A pregnancy test," Devon mumbled beneath her breath.

"A what—?" Kate gasped, her stomach flipping again. "I'm not..."

"Are you sure? Like *sure*, sure?" Devon glared at her. "Remember when Morgan was convinced she had some fatal disease because she was in denial? This is looking a whole lot like that."

Devon drew a big circle in the air around Kate, who simply gawked.

"I'm having déjà motherfucking vu." Devon leaned her hip up against the counter and grinned. "Look, I'm just a construction worker, not a doctor. But if I had a hundred dollars in my pocket right now, I'd bet it all on you being knocked up."

Kate did some quick mental math and couldn't make it compute. When was the last time she'd had her period? She couldn't quickly recall, but maybe it was the shock of the bomb Devon had dropped on her. Could she be right?

"I would ordinarily call one of the guys to get us a test plus ten spares for when you don't believe that first one, but..." Devon shrugged.

Kate winced. "Yeah. Don't do that."

They both remembered the time Joe had gone out for a box and Dave had gotten in his near-fatal wreck. It was bad juju to even bring it up.

"So will you be okay if I leave for a few minutes?" Devon asked.

"Yeah, yeah. I'm fine. As long as I don't move. And don't go in the kitchen. And..." Kate pinched the bridge of her nose. Was it her imagination or was her chest still aching, and maybe not from Mike pinning her to the wall the night before.

"Right. Well, I'm going to the drugstore down the street. I will be back in five minutes. If you're gonna hurl, do it while I'm gone, huh?" Devon teased because she understood Kate well enough to know that alone would steel her guts and make sure she fought the wave of illness threatening her as she considered the possibilities.

Could it be true?

Her kids were well out of the infant phase. Would she even know how to start over?

A baby would change everything.

Again.

5

Kate tapped her fingers on the steering wheel of her car. She'd never driven this far by herself before, especially without Mike knowing what she was up to. He would probably be pissed, but she'd been careful. Plus, the rest of the crew were well aware of where she was going and when to expect her call telling them that she'd arrived safely.

Besides, he'd get over it when she informed him of her big, and still unbelievable, news.

She rested her hand low on her stomach. As the miles rolled away, she took the chance to really think about everything for the first time. With Morgan and Joe in Middletown for at least the entire summer, and probably longer, she was going to have to figure out how to be pregnant on her own.

Sure, the rest of the crew would be there, but neither Kayla nor Devon had ever wanted kids and they couldn't understand what she was about to go through the same way Morgan always had. Both of the other times she'd done this, Morgan had been pregnant too. They'd been inseparable since elementary school and, somehow, going through this without the support of her best friend seemed nearly impossible. Especially now that she was older and things were riskier.

Phone calls and video chats could only do so much when you needed a hug.

Speaking of, she could sure use one of those. Thankfully, she realized with a slow blink, she was only about twenty miles away from Hot Rods. The past several hours had flown by as she reflected on her fears, the blossoming joy and hope that she was almost afraid to embrace, and the anticipation of letting Mike in on her secret.

Kate turned into the parking lot beside the Hot Rods garage. She turned off the car, then sat there, staring through the trees at the clearing that hadn't been there last time she'd visited. The land had already been leveled and the outline of a multistory structure rose up from the forest.

Wow, that was going to be a hell of an upgrade for the Hot Rods gang.

No wonder Joe was freaking out about getting it right. This was an even bigger opportunity for him than she'd fully realized.

Hopefully she'd done the right thing by coming there and interrupting. The familiar whir of power tools from both the garage beside her and the site out back calmed her. But she obviously sat there a little too long. Someone must have noticed, because a familiar form materialized on the path out of the woods.

Despite the mottled shade falling on him, she knew it was Mike right away. His determined, long-legged strides, the way he whipped his hardhat off and stowed it under his arm, and his favorite red work shirt tucked into sexy-as-hell ripped jeans—yep, she would recognize her husband anywhere.

"Kate?" Mike shouted as he raced toward her car. She hadn't even climbed out or stretched her legs when he came bounding to meet her. "What are you doing here? Is everything okay?"

"Yeah." She smiled. He steadied her as she unfolded herself, then stood and held her arms out for the reassuring embrace she so desperately needed right then. "Things are...great, actually. I mean, I think they are."

But would he agree?

"Where are Abby and Landry?" Mike asked, peering into the empty backseat of the car. "Did you bring them too?"

"No. Dave and Kayla have them at the resort. They're making an adventure out of this week, staying in that tree house cabin you guys built at Bare Natural after being inspired by Kason's place last year." Kate smiled, remembering how excited the kids had been about the sudden turn of events. Hell, the way their eyes had lit up, she and Mike should have taken them out there sooner for a family getaway. It was probably the only thing that could have gotten Abby to forgive her for not bringing her to see Nathan sooner than the weekend, when they were all set to meet up again. "I thought it would be better if I came alone."

"Why?" Mike drew her close. "Not that I'm not excited to see you. I'm thrilled. I just figured if you decided to join me, you'd have the kids with you. It must have been impossible to keep Abby from visiting Nathan. Unless this isn't just about missing me or wanting to visit with Morgan and Joe a little longer this week...is it?"

"Those are great things, too. They are. But they're not why I came." Kate swallowed hard, trying to figure out some magazine-worthy way to divulge her motivation for the trip. But that took planning and effort and damn she was tired...and nervous.

"What's wrong?" Mike held her shoulders and extended his arms so he could peer into her eyes.

"Nothing, I promise. Do you need to go back up to the site? Maybe we can talk about this later, in private?" Kate lifted her chin as more people began to stream out of the woods, from the Hot Rods garage, and from the adorable cabin where Joe's uncle Tom lived. Pretty soon they were going to be swarmed by well-meaning friends.

"Joe can handle that stuff." Mike waved her off. "Whether he doubts it or not, he has things under control. And I don't care who hears our dirty laundry. If something's messed up, tell me so I can fix it."

If he only knew that he'd already taken care of her a little too well.

"Well, look who's here!" Uncle Tom boomed as he and his wife, Ms. Brown—who would always be Ms. Brown to them all despite having married Tom—joined them. His son, Eli, ambled out onto the blacktop, wiping grease on a rag tucked into the waistband of his jumpsuit. Alanso and Sally were, as usual, close behind him.

"Kate!" Ms. Brown reached her first, enveloping her in a warm hug that brought tears to Kate's eyes. Yup, pregnancy hormones...check! "This is a lovely surprise. Did Mike know you were coming?"

"Ummm, nope." Kate bit her lower lip and tried not to wring her hands.

"So what's the special occasion?" Tom asked as he piled on to Ms. Brown, enveloping them both in his strong, reassuring hold. Kate could have stayed there forever. She understood why Joe was drawn to this place and these people and the possibility of a true family, even if it wasn't exactly the one he'd been born into. Tom and Ms. Brown had become parental figures for them all. She squeezed them back, and if they noticed her trembling in their grasp, they didn't rat her out and only held her tighter.

"That's a very good question." Mike swept his gaze over Kate from her eyes to the tips of her sneakers as if he could find a clue written on her somewhere.

Kate almost seized the chance then, but before she could, not only Eli, Alanso, and Sally appeared, but also Joe, then Sabra and Holden chasing their twin sons, who were shouting, "Is Landry here? Can he play with us?"

Soon Kate was taking turns hugging what seemed like a million people, and yet she felt guilty because her husband was staring at her in concern, trying to wait for her to finish greeting them all, though he wasn't exactly the patient-type.

"Shouldn't you be a bit happier to see your wife, buddy?" Roman teased with a light elbow to Mike's ribs. "If Carver drove five hundred miles to see me, I'd be a bit more excited. Especially since she left the kids at home, you know what I mean?"

"Shit, sorry. I'm thrilled to see you," Mike promised her, then frowned before addressing Roman. "I'm still trying to pry whatever my wife came here to tell me out of her."

"Oh shit, we're interrupting." Carver, Roman's husband, grabbed his arm and tugged, walking a few steps backward toward the garage.

"No, no. It's okay." Kate blinked. But was it? Suddenly

it seemed like she'd made a terrible decision. What if Mike didn't want the baby? What if she embarrassed him by dropping this bomb in front of all the people they cared about? It got harder to breathe.

"Are you *sure* you're okay?" he asked, stepping closer and extending his hand toward her.

"Yeah," she replied reflexively. Except she wasn't.

Surrounded by so many people—their warmth and the pressure of their attention on her—she overheated. The world tipped and Kate's eyes blurred. She probably should have drunk some more water on the drive, but she hadn't wanted to stop to pee too often and delay getting there until after dark. If it hadn't been for her husband, she might have crashed to the ground.

But he proved again that he would never let her fall. She sagged, ending up plastered against his chest.

The crowd around them went silent, pretty much a miracle.

She drew several deep breaths until the world stopped turning too fast and she could find her footing again.

"What the hell is going on, Kate?" Mike was going to lose his shit if she didn't find some way to convince him she was okay.

So she opted for the truth. Looking at the concerned and familiar faces surrounding them, she didn't mind sharing the moment with everyone. They were family, in the broadest sense of the word. Hopefully Mike wouldn't care either. "I wanted to think of some clever way to tell you but, uh, I'm sort of pregnant."

"What?" Mike blinked at her.

"Sort of?" Uncle Tom unleashed a giant belly laugh at that. "It's been a while since I heard those words directed at me, but as far as I remember, it's not a *sort of* condition."

Ms. Brown smacked him lightly with the back of her hand. "Tommy. Shush."

"Oh my God, that's amazing news." Sally, who was also pregnant, sniffled then crushed Kate between her and Mike. "Congratulations, you two!"

And yet, Mike still stood there, frozen. "A...a baby? Like a miniature person. That kind of baby."

Kate nodded a few times quickly, but not enough that she'd get dizzy again.

"You're having a baby?" Mike asked as he brushed a strand of hair away from her eyes so that he could look directly into them.

"*We're* having a baby," she answered.

"Hang out here a while and your kid can be besties with Eli's." Holden grinned. "Might as well share baby shit and sitters while you're at it. We have no shortage of those around here, you know."

Stay? In Middletown? Kate peeked over Mike's shoulder at the construction site and the future Joe and now Mike too for a little while at least, were building here. It was only supposed to be temporary but...

Then again, what if Mike didn't even want another child? Maybe she should have waited and told him once they were alone, but she couldn't hold the secret in even one more second when she'd remembered how tiny their children had looked in his big, strong, capable hands. And how much he loved them.

Kate's breath froze in her lungs. What if he didn't want this? New beginnings at their age could be terrifying. Look at what Joe and Morgan had gone through to reach for theirs. And that had been progress, not going back to where they'd been over ten years ago.

Mike took one more ragged breath and then he was

there, his hands cupping her face as he smiled, slow and wide until all she could see was pure, unadulterated bliss. The same sort she'd felt since she realized that what she'd been denying was true. They were doing this again, whether they'd planned to or not.

He murmured, "I love you."

But instead of kissing her like she expected, Mike sank to his knees. His hands cradled her hips this time while his thumbs brushed over her belly. "And I love you. How can I love someone I didn't even know existed until a moment ago? I don't know, but I can't wait to meet you, little baby."

Then he buried his face in her shirt as if he couldn't stand to be even an inch away from the life growing inside her.

It wasn't until he rose and she saw the tears dampening his cheeks that she totally lost her shit, practically trying to climb him. With his arms banded around her, everything in her world was perfect. She had no idea where they would go from there, but as long as they were together, and they had their children, they would be just fine.

"Now that's a hell of a surprise," Joe teased as he put one hand each on Mike and Kate.

Holden and Sabra, Roman and Carver, Uncle Tom and Ms. Brown, and all the rest of the Hot Rods piled on for an epic group hug. Kate wished the rest of the Powertools were there to share the moment with them, but the next best thing was having their Hot Rods cousins join in the celebrations.

"Wow, this is incredible." Mike looked as dazed as she'd felt when she'd finally accepted what the entire box of tests Devon had bought her had said. "I don't even know how this happened. I mean, we're careful and..."

"Oh, I know how it happened." Kaige, another one of the mechanics, grinned before thrusting the wrench in his hand through the circle of his thumb and forefinger.

"What does that mean?" one of Holden's sons asked.

"Nothing!" Sabra shot Kaige a glare, then smiled sweetly. "Uncle Kaige will explain it to you and Ambrose someday, won't you?"

When Kaige considered educating his daughter about the birds and the bees, his smirk vanished. "In about fifty years, sure."

Everyone laughed at that, Kate included.

"Man, I can't wait to see Morgan's face when you tell her. She's going to be so happy for you." Joe clapped Mike on the shoulder.

Kate saw the moment it dawned on him, just as it had her...

"But we're going to be here at least all summer." Joe looked from his cousin, Eli, who was about to be a first-time dad, then to Mike and back—panic, dread, obligation, all of it warring with joy and excitement in his warm eyes, causing them to crinkle at the corners.

"It's okay," Kate hurried to reassure him. "Look at what you're doing here—Eli needs you. You were right to come. This is obviously a huge opportunity for you and Morgan too."

"If you need to go home, we'll figure this out." Eli was quick to let Joe off the hook, but anyone who knew Joe knew he wasn't capable of backing down from responsibility.

"No, no." Joe ran his hands through his hair. "I'm not bailing on you. I just, wow. Mike isn't going to be able to be away from home, so he'll need to teach me everything he knows this week. And kids all around. It's going to be a really fun year, huh?"

Uncle Tom came forward, putting one hand on Eli's shoulder and the other on Joe's. Then he took an extra step and surrounded both Mike and Kate in another of his famous bear hugs. "You two should take the rest of the afternoon off. Go celebrate. I'm sure you have a lot to talk about. The rest will work itself out. You'll see."

"That's a good idea." Joe nodded. "I think I can manage not to fuck shit up if you get out of here for a few hours."

Mike huffed. "Cut that out. You don't need me."

But the reality was that in the crew, they all needed each other. Being separated was going to be harder than they'd imagined. They'd have to figure out a way to make it work.

Just thinking about it sapped the last of Kate's strength. She had to find somewhere quiet to snuggle in her husband's arms so she could figure out if he really was as happy as she was to be going on this adventure in parenthood with him, one more time.

Mike noticed and scooped her into his arms, not waiting for her to collapse again. He nodded to everyone and said, "I'll see you all tomorrow, and you when you get off work tonight."

He jerked his chin at Joe, who nodded.

That's right! Kate remembered Mike was staying with Joe and Morgan as he deposited her in the passenger seat of her car and clicked her seatbelt into place. Then he jogged around to the driver's side and moved the seat back what seemed like ten notches before joining her. She waved to everyone as they shouted congratulations and warm wishes.

Mike's fingers entwined with hers. The heat and strength in his grasp drew the last of her nervous energy from her, and before she realized it, she'd closed her eyes. The pretty moss-colored light filtering through the canopy above as they wound through the woods toward Morgan and Joe's rental house was the last thing she remembered before she dozed off.

6

"Is it true? Is it true?"

Mike was only half awake when someone, a woman from the feel of her soft body, piled on top of him and Kate where they'd been dozing after she'd made her announcement at Hot Rods. The revelation rushed back in to his awakening mind. A baby! They were having another baby. Whoa.

"Morgan?" Kate scrubbed her eyes and blinked up at her best friend, a wide smile spreading across her face as she hugged the other woman.

Mike stretched and looked up at Joe. He grinned at his wife, who'd wedged herself between Mike and Kate in bed. Hell, it wasn't like they hadn't slept together a hundred times in the past fourteen years or so. Joe rounded the carved four-poster and sat on the edge of the mattress behind Kate.

"Yeah, it's me. So tell me." Morgan put her hand on Kate's stomach. "It's not some kind of joke, right?"

"Nope." Kate beamed, looking more gorgeous than ever. "I'm pregnant."

Hearing the words from his wife stole Mike's breath all over again. It seemed like some kind of dream. A nice one, though. He'd be lying if he said he didn't look at Abby and see the woman she'd be in another few blinks of his eye. He missed having little ones around. A child who actually needed him and enjoyed the attention he paid to the adorable things they did. But now he'd have not only Eli's kid and some of the others at Hot Rides to spoil when he saw them on occasion, but his own to raise day in and day out.

It was overwhelming to think of starting fresh, but also exciting.

Maybe Joe had been right to consider moving to Middletown and doing things differently than they had been for so long now. Sure, the years they'd been a crew had been awesome. So good that they hadn't had any desire to shake things up. But they'd gotten stale. Things had become routine. Maybe they'd settled for good enough when they could have pushed for greatness.

If Mike was going to give his kid the life he wanted for him or her, he might have to think about what else needed to change and evolve. He should be setting an example for Abby, Landry, and now this new baby. Seeing the scale of the Hot Rods project and the additional challenges and prosperity an operation of that magnitude could bring, Mike was already buzzing with ideas for new opportunities.

As he surrounded his wife and her best friend—both giddy with joy—in his arms, he wondered if staying in Middletown longer than a week or even a summer might be best for the four of them.

"Oh my God!" Morgan sniffled and Kate wiped a tear

from her cheek. "That's such incredible news. I'm so happy for you. Were you trying...?"

Mike squeezed Morgan and Kate. This might be a bit of a sensitive subject for Morgan and Joe since they'd struggled so hard to have their first child and had been blessed unexpectedly with a second. They might have opted for more if fate had permitted, and here he and Kate were having one by chance.

"No." Kate yawned and sat up a bit, reaching one hand out to Joe, who patted her fingers then enfolded them in his own. "You know I would have told you if we decided something that life-changing. It just happened."

She got quieter then and looked away, out the giant windows overlooking the pristine lawn that stretched down a rolling hill toward the dark, loamy onion fields streaked with green that lined the valley in the distance.

"You okay?" Morgan wormed against Mike until she could see Kate's face. He tried not to notice how warm and soft and pretty she was, his wife's best friend, who was also sometimes his lover. But when he looked up at Joe, whose mouth was tipped up on one side, he knew his friend was not oblivious to the effects the two women had on either of them, which were magnified when they were together.

"It's just freaking me out a little, to think of doing this by myself." Kate bit her lower lip. "I know Mike might need to be up here helping Joe sometimes, and that's fine. Totally fine."

She held Joe's hand tighter.

"But the other two times I did this, you were doing it too. With me." Kate cursed under her breath. "Sorry. That's selfish and I don't mean to hurt your feelings because I know you always hoped you might get lucky again..."

"Hey, it's fine. I promise." Morgan chuckled then. "Dirty diapers and baby proofing a house and all that... I think I'm beyond that stage of life."

"What if we are too?" Kate looked past Morgan to Mike. "Are we really ready to do this again? And on our own? I mean...you won't be there, will you, Morgan? Even after the summer. Look at this place. I can see how happy you are here. You're not coming home, are you?"

Morgan looked to Joe then. They both frowned. Morgan took a deep breath. "I'm not sure, Kate. We haven't been out here that long, but it's hard to deny that it feels like it could be somewhere we belong. Joe is going to find his footing with the foreman thing, I know it. Especially with Mike coaching him for a bit. And Devra and I have been talking about some really exciting plans. There's a small storefront for rent near hers. With the cost of living here, a lot more things are possible..."

She looked up at Joe. "Sorry, I was going to talk to you about that the other day, but then the accident happened and I wasn't sure if it was the right time and..."

"Wow." Mike looked at Morgan and Joe and his guts twisted a bit. This was it. They weren't coming home. He believed, as Morgan did, that Joe only needed a bit of time to gain his confidence. Then he'd be ready to lead and to grow his own business. "Yeah, I mean, Joe would be a dumbass to give this up just to come back and work for me. Look at where you are. It's gorgeous. And if there are real prospects for you here, plus family, you'd be foolish to give that up."

"You don't want me back?" Joe asked.

"Shut the fuck up, idiot." Mike would have punched

his shoulder if he could have reached across their wives. "Of course I do. But that doesn't mean I'm blind. I can see why this would work for you and how you've outgrown us."

When he looked up again, both Kate and Morgan had glassy eyes. If they started bawling he'd lose it too, and he didn't want any of them getting that upset, Kate especially, on one of the happiest days of his life.

"We can talk more about this shit later." Mike sat up and hauled Morgan and Kate into his lap, playfully crushing them both to him before laying a smacking kiss on each of their temples. "Why don't you guys give us the official tour? I didn't see much when I carried Kate up here, and she was already passed out. After that we can call the crew."

"Good idea." Kate turned her head for a proper kiss, then squeezed Morgan one more time before rolling toward Joe, who helped her climb out of the enormous, comfortable bed in the guest suite of the house he and Morgan were renting.

"This is incredible." Mike whistled as Joe and Morgan showed them around. It was becoming more and more obvious that this had been a one-way trip for the couple, even if they weren't ready to admit that to themselves yet.

"Land and material costs are so much less expensive out here, we could build something like this and cover the mortgage with what we could get in rent for Morgan's apartment back home."

"No shit." Mike wondered if they might need to consider some similar options. After all, with a baby on the way, a freaking baby, they were going to have to rebuild a nursery and set up a room separate from his two older kids, which they didn't have space for in their current house.

Maybe if they renovated the attic...

"Yeah, it's pretty sweet, right?" Joe turned toward him. "Imagine what we could do if we built a place like this ourselves. All the little details we could add and how special we could make it. I talked to Uncle Tom about maybe scoping out a bit of the Hot Rods land I could buy from him. You know that sweet spot down near the lake?"

"Oh, hell yeah." Mike was getting more envious by the second. "So that means you're really considering staying, right?"

"Just trying to weigh the options." Joe glanced away, guilty as fuck. It was easy to see where his heart was. And though it might be torn in two, he was leaning this way. If his bio family and his family by choice were equal weights on the scale of his life, then something like a house like this, better pay—with college not too far off for his kids—and a long-term plan for his retirement, could be what tipped him in favor of Middletown.

Mike couldn't blame the man for pursuing happiness. It sounded pretty damn good to him too.

"Check this out." Joe ushered them through the showroom-worthy kitchen into a glass four-season room. Hedges surrounded the yard and rosebushes bloomed along the entire perimeter. Every possible shade of green and pink was reflected off the walls. It was calming and serene.

Mike instantly felt better. He sank onto one of the loveseats and pulled Kate into his lap. "Mind if we just sit here for a few minutes? It's so peaceful."

"Yeah, of course. There's still the whole lower level to see too, but it's mostly a play area for the kids. A hangout spot to watch movies, and games, and stuff. Or, you know, to have crew meetings. There are a bunch of couches and wide-open space."

"Damn, I see why you like it here." Mike stroked Kate's side, sighing when she melted into him. "It would be a great place to raise a family. It's a lot newer than our houses and way less cramped. I guess we need to start thinking about logistics too."

Kate stiffened as if she hadn't considered that. Hell, this had to be as much of a shock to her as it was to him.

"It's okay, we'll make it work even if we need to get creative," he promised her.

"So you're happy about the baby? Really?" Kate whispered to him while staring into his eyes, as if to detect even the faintest flicker of doubt. There was none to spot.

"Of course I am." He kissed her so that she could taste his enthusiasm even if she doubted what she saw. "I love you. Our family is the most important thing in the world to me. Making it bigger... Well, I didn't expect it, but yeah, I'm thrilled."

"Then what's this frown about?" she murmured before she kissed the side of his mouth gently, soothingly.

"He's worried about you," Morgan answered for him. And she wasn't wrong.

"Yeah. I mean, Morgan is your best friend, and we've always had each other to rely on. Kayla and Dave and Devon, James and Neil are awesome. But they're not kid people and I don't want to lean too much on them. This isn't what they chose for themselves, so why would they want to deal with our family all the time?"

"Don't let them hear you talking like that." Joe snickered. "Someone will knee you in the nuts."

"Well, don't fucking snitch then." Mike rolled his eyes.

"It's just different." Morgan reached out and put her hand on Mike's. "I know what you mean. I'm worried about Kate too. I wish I could be there while she was going through the pregnancy."

"It's not going to be easier now that I'm older, is it?" Kate nibbled on her lower lip, glancing between her husband and her best friend.

"Sorry, I didn't mean to stress you out." Morgan leaned over and hugged Kate. "You're going to do great. I just feel like a shitty friend because I won't be there for all of it. Or maybe any of it. Things have been feeling...right here."

"At least until the accident. Which makes it even worse. I'm probably not cut out for this." Joe scrunched his eyes closed and leaned forward. "Sorry, Morgan. Don't get your heart set on all this yet. I might not be able to pull it off."

"You will," Kate, Morgan, and Mike insisted together.

"I'm glad you three are so sure." Joe slumped in the chair facing Mike and Kate's, prompting Morgan to curl up in his lap. The couples mirrored each other.

"Look, we don't have all the answers yet." Mike sighed and hugged Kate. "But lots of good things are happening. Maybe we should take a few minutes to be grateful. We can deal with the rest as it comes. For right now, I'm proud of you and Morgan for trying something new and thrilled to maybe be doing some of that myself with Kate and this baby."

"I like the sound of that. And in case I haven't said it lately, Joe, I'm proud of you too." Morgan leaned in and kissed Joe while Mike did the same to his wife. He lost track of time as they settled in to something a hell of a lot more comfortable and familiar. Stress leached out of his muscles as Kate melted in his arms then shifted so that she straddled him. Her foot bumped Morgan's calf as her best friend did exactly the same yet facing the opposite direction.

And before Mike knew it, he and Joe each had a lapful of their gorgeous, very willing, very wonderful wives. Now this he was thankful for. He'd been craving the crew connection, especially the bond between the four of them, since Joe and Morgan had left for this assignment. No reason he shouldn't take advantage of where they'd ended up.

7

When Kate reached down and grabbed the hem of Mike's shirt, wrestling it up his abs, he leaned forward and got rid of it for her, happy to have it gone. Joe's landed on top of where he tossed it on the floor. Morgan hummed in appreciation and stroked her husband's chest. Although Kate couldn't see like Mike could, she did the same to him. They were so in tune, they acted as one unit instead of two couples.

Kate kissed him, letting him cup her ass and relish the feeling of having her there, on top of him, warm and sweet. And when she glanced over her shoulder and said, "Hey, Morgan, want to have a contest?"

Morgan practically purred as she looked over. "What are you thinking?"

"Let's suck them off. Whichever one of us makes them about to lose control first gets to have them both." Kate flexed her fingers on Mike's shoulders, scoring him with her nails. He didn't mind in the least.

"You know I'm always up for a bet. But...I did have all

the guys last time," Morgan demurred. "And it's your special day. Let's get them good and ready and then you can have them both. I'm sure Joe will take care of me after."

"Go back to the part where you go down on us." Joe speared his fingers into his wife's long, wavy brown hair. "I liked that part."

"Me too." Mike slapped Kate's ass. "And you're right, Morgan. You know we'll always take care of you. Both of you."

"I mostly just wanted to watch you two duke it out," Kate muttered. "I love it when you get lost in pleasure."

"Same goes." He guided her down until she knelt between his knees, and spread his legs wider. "Don't worry, I plan on turning the tables soon enough."

"I'm counting on it." She traced the ridge of his erection through his pants with the tip of a single nail before opening his jeans and peeling them down his legs.

Morgan did the same to Joe.

And as one, the women stood. Back to back, they stripped for their men, and maybe in some way for each other, because no one could deny how powerful they were in that moment. They had Mike and Joe's rapt attention. By the time Kate was down to her lacy briefs and Morgan was wearing one of the skimpiest thongs Mike had ever seen, he wondered if she would even get his dick in her mouth before he tapped out. His cock ached for her touch, and the slick heat of her lips wrapped around it.

"You going to look at it all day or are you going to suck it?" he teased, knowing she'd make him pay for it. And that he'd love every second.

Kate looked over her shoulder at Morgan. They shared

a grin before sinking to their knees. Neither of them rushed, though. They took their time, teasing their husbands with light caresses over their balls and the underside of their shafts. Finally, Kate glanced up at him and said, "Count it down."

"Hmm?" Mike had already forgotten everything except the fact that she was about to suck him off.

"The contest. Starts in three...two...one. Go!" Thankfully Joe still had a couple brain cells left unoccupied by visions of his wife swallowing him whole. That didn't bode well for Mike's chances. Usually he could out-stamina the rest of the crew. But maybe not today when he was on the edge, concerned with the future and what it held for their group.

Hell, maybe he'd been like this for months. Ever since he first sensed something different about Joe, and the changes brewing for them all.

But right then every thought went out of his mind except holding on for his wife, so that he could give her what she so clearly desired. The first contact of her lips on his dick were as unsubtle as a lightning strike. It lit every nerve ending in his body up like the massive Christmas tree Devon, Neil, and James insisted on putting up at Bare Natural each year.

Fortunately it seemed like Joe was suffering a similar blow. Over Kate's head, Mike watched Morgan take Joe's cock into her mouth, humming as she swallowed most of him in a single long glide. He might have been smug, knowing Joe wouldn't be able to resist that sort of treatment for long, except that it was so hot it ratcheted Mike's own rapture up a notch or ten.

He dug his fingers into the arm of the white wicker

chair, easing up only when it creaked in his grip. Kate smiled smugly around his dick and began to work his shaft, lapping at the base before pulling off and swirling her tongue around the head.

She knew every millimeter of him and exactly where her efforts would have the best payoff.

Unsurprisingly, Morgan had the same intimate knowledge of Joe.

It wasn't long before Joe's ragged breathing became apparent and he dropped his head back with a groan. Mike couldn't let him win. He looked down at Kate and saw all the things he loved about her, her playfulness, her determination, her skill, and her innate seductiveness.

His balls drew tight and a spurt of precome shot from his dick.

Mike slapped his palm on his thigh. "That's it. Stop or I'm going to come in your mouth."

"And we know from the baby situation that that's not how you two roll," Morgan said with a smirk as she delicately wiped her mouth with the back of her hand.

"You didn't go easy on Joe for my sake, did you?" Kate glared at her best friend.

Joe's deep red cheeks said otherwise. Mike almost felt bad for the man. Except that he knew how much better things were about to get. If Kate wanted them both, he'd be happy to share her, satisfy her, and then make sure Morgan didn't go without either. There were plenty of ways to please them both, and he took his responsibility as the foreman seriously.

Mike wouldn't let them down.

Kate surprised him when she rose and straddled him once again. This time her soaked pussy slid along his shaft. It wouldn't take more than a twitch for him to be buried inside her. She asked her friend, "Morgan?"

"Yeah?"

"Mind if I claim my prize later? I'm suddenly hungry for just one thing." Kate shrugged. "Pregnancy cravings. They're weird like that."

"You can always have a rain check," Joe promised as Morgan sighed and climbed into her husband's lap.

"I'm never going to turn down a chance to take you for a ride either." Morgan patted Joe on his still-heaving chest. Mike had a feeling this wasn't going to be some kind of drawn-out affair.

Or at least it might not have been if his phone hadn't rung at just that instant.

"Ignore it." Joe glared at Mike. "There's no one who needs your attention more than us right now."

It was Kate who hesitated, though. "Wait. Just make sure it's not one of the kids, okay?"

Mike nodded and fished his phone out of his discarded pants pocket. He groaned when he saw it was Dave calling. "Either it's something about the kids or work shit or this is going to be a hell of a lot more fun anyway."

Joe grinned. "Answer it. Hurry up. Even if it is the kids, we can keep the crew on the line after they're gone. I probably need a few seconds to get my shit together anyway."

Morgan's mouth curled up at that. She dragged her finger across his parted lips. "Liked that, did you?"

Just as Mike connected, Joe answered, "Fuck yes."

"Um, what exactly is going on there?" Dave asked. "And how long can you wait for us to drive out and join you?"

"Oh, hey." Mike cleared his throat and tried to sound like he wasn't two seconds away from burying himself in Kate's lush body. "What do you need?"

"*Need*?" Dave grumbled, "Nothing. But we couldn't stand waiting to hear from you assholes anymore. Kate got there, right? She's okay? And she told you..."

"Oh, shit!" Kate went ramrod straight in his arms, risking making their current child the last one they were capable of having.

He guided her knee safely away from his groin.

"I forgot to call. I'm so sorry. Things were...intense when I arrived, and then I passed out. Literally and then for a nap and..."

"You what?" Devon asked.

Kate shrugged it off. "Nothing serious. I got overwhelmed for a second."

"As long as you're okay, it's fine." Dave chuckled. "I'm glad you're safe and everyone is happy. You all right, Mike?"

"I'm ecstatic." Mike's chest puffed up as he thought again about how they were about to expand their family. "We were about to celebrate. I'm sorry I didn't think of calling you to join us."

"Exactly what kind of party are you having?" Neil wondered.

"Are we on speaker phone?" Mike asked.

"Yeah, but there aren't any little ears around, if that's what you're worried about," Devon added. "We're still at the job site. Abby and Landry are with Kayla up at the resort. They might never come down from that tree house, just so you know."

Kate smiled at that. "I'm glad they're having fun. I felt so bad leaving them, but..."

"You couldn't get to Mike fast enough," James said with a sigh. "We know, Katiebug."

"Maybe I can make up for leaving you guys with all that grunt work," Mike suggested. "Let's turn this into a video conference..."

8

When Mike suggested they let their friends see what they were up to, Kate practically purred and rubbed up against him. He never would have imagined it when he'd first met the shy young neighbor who'd recently inherited the property next to one of their projects, but over the years she'd developed quite a thing for allowing people to watch her get him off even as she let go herself.

At least these people, whom she knew and loved and trusted.

The years they'd spent together had ensured their bond was unbreakable. Or at least he'd thought so until recently. Maybe it was time to reinforce it and show them all how strong it really was, even if they weren't in the same city at the moment.

"Tell me we're about to see some tits and ass." Neil sounded like he might be high-fiving either Dave or James, or hell, maybe Devon, who sometimes was into that too, though usually with Kayla, not Morgan or Kate.

Mike looked around. Joe, Morgan, and Kate smiled

back, definitely not reaching for anything to cover up with.

"Do it. Just hurry," Kate rasped. "I've already lost some of my patience."

"Since when have you had any?" Morgan teased. "You never do when it comes to Mike's cock."

Mike tapped the camera button and allowed his phone to start transmitting video. As soon as the half of their crew on the other end saw what was going on in Joe and Morgan's sunroom, they started to undress.

Neil had his shirt off when he squinted at the screen. "Does that whole room have leaded glass windows?"

"Are you seriously looking at the fucking windows right now?" Mike growled. "I should hang up on you."

"Don't! Don't do that." Dave smacked Neil in the gut with the back of his mammoth hand. "Aim the phone a little more to the right, though. So we can see more of you guys and be less distracted by the architectural details."

"Ohhh, that's a much better view." James hummed. "Nice lighting with the sparkles from the bevels in those fancy-as fuck-windows I definitely did not notice as much as you four hanging out surrounded by them while naked."

Kate laughed. "Good to know. Now, if you don't mind, we were about to get to the good stuff. So can you please catch up?"

"Yeah, what she said." Morgan rocked against Joe, probably rubbing her clit against his erection to keep herself hyped up.

Joe's hands flew to her ass, guiding her up and down. The motion spread her cheeks and gave Mike all sorts of wicked ideas for later. He took the phone and propped it up on the windowsill nearby. "How's that? Can you still see? I need my hands for more important stuff."

He ran them up and down Kate's back, scratching light circles there, which never failed to set her off. Sure enough, she reached for his cock.

"We can see just fine. So go ahead, show us what you were up to." Neil shucked his jeans as Dave, Devon, and James finished getting naked too. Boots clunked onto the wooden floors as the crew headed into the living room. They'd left the mattress Dave had put there after Joe had told them of his plans to come out to Middletown.

In that moment, Mike had never imagined he might be far away too, soon. Especially not with his life changing at least as drastically as the other guy's had lately. But as he sat there in the glistening sunlight with his wife and the couple beside him, he couldn't say it felt wrong either.

Mike looked at Kate, who grinned, then to Joe, who didn't wait to swoop in on Morgan. The guys shifted gears. Sure, letting their wives play was fun, but this...this was what they did best. Mike pressed Kate to the soft carpet and blanketed her with his body, being more careful than he might have been before she'd shared her news with him and rocked his world. The other times, they'd been trying, he'd expected it. This...was a shock. Like winning the lottery when he hadn't even bought a ticket.

"I hope you enjoyed teasing us," he rubbed the stubble on his chin over her cheek before nibbling on her ear.

"Because now it's our turn." Joe reached over and fist-bumped Mike before crushing his mouth to Morgan's. Where things had been flirty and fun before, they were suddenly more serious as the rest of the crew observed.

Mike never could explain why this worked for them or

the extra edge it lent their sex lives, but it was undeniable that whether they were in the same city or not, they shared a connection that enriched all of their lives.

Relief added to arousal as he realized that no matter where they were, they would always have this. Someway, somehow, they would stay a crew. One that played and loved together even if it wasn't in the same ways they'd done it before. They were capable of growing—of evolving—without breaking apart.

He looked over his shoulder at his phone and barked, "You perverts aren't just going to sit there and watch us fuck, are you? I want to hear how much you're enjoying the show."

"Hell yeah, foreman," Dave sounded off. "You don't have to tell me twice."

The rustle coming from the direction of the phone guaranteed he was settling into place on the mattress. Some people took coffee breaks; the crew liked to blow off steam with an entirely different vice. It worked for them, bringing them closer and chilling them out when they were under the pressure of deadlines and the physical demands of manual labor. After all, an epic orgasm was even better at unknotting muscles than one of Kayla's infamous massages.

Mike kissed Kate, knowing the display they were putting on would inspire their friends to treat each other to the same simple pleasures. Well, at least that's how they'd start out. And sure enough, it wasn't long before he heard soft moans not only from Joe and Morgan beside him, but from Devon, Neil, James, and Dave back home.

He checked on them long enough to see that Dave was making out with Neil as James and Devon did the same before switching off between them. There was an awful lot of bare, tanned flesh on display too. When he turned his attention back to Kate, he caught her peeking over his shoulder.

"You like what you see?" he asked.

She nodded. "You should call me next time you guys decide to do this at work."

"Me too," Morgan added on a gasp. "Why haven't we thought of that before? I always wonder what you're up to."

"Today you don't have to imagine. You get the real thing." Mike smiled down at Kate and rubbed up against her, his dick sliding over her mound. He loved how slick she was already. He didn't have to ask if she was up for it —she made that clear with her ragged breathing and her nails digging into his shoulders—but he did anyway. "Is this okay?"

"No. It won't be okay until you're inside me. Fuck, Mike. I'm so horny I'm going to die if you don't do it soon." She clawed at his back.

"I did notice that the other day, outside, too." Mike chuckled. "I think I like you pregnant. Maybe we should do this another couple of times."

"What'd we miss?" Neil asked. "That sounds like fun."

"It was something like this..." Mike took his cock in hand and fed it into his wife. The first contact of her hot pussy on his shaft took his breath away every damn time. And this one was no exception. "Except faster, and harder, and up against the exterior wall of our house in broad daylight."

"Damn." Joe nuzzled Morgan's neck and must have followed Mike's lead because his wife gasped then hummed, her ankles locking in the small of Joe's back. "I knew we were missing the good stuff while we were out here."

"Not now you're not," Mike told him. Their gazes collided for a moment before their attention returned to their wives and the pleasure they brought each other.

Someone—Devon, he thought—moaned from the other side of the phone. She confirmed it when she begged, "I need someone to fuck me too. Please, hurry."

"I've got you," James promised. "If Neil has me."

"Hell yes. I do," Neil said.

"And I've got you," Dave added. The smack that followed was likely a slap on Neil's ass as the four crew members lined up to please each other in one long train of passion.

"Oh God, that's hot." Morgan spread her legs wider, her knee nudging Mike's hip as she made as much room as possible for Joe to plow into her. "No wonder you guys love working together."

"We don't fuck around all of the time," Devon promised with a snort that dissolved into something like a gasp. Mike knew that noise and could picture James sinking into her, distracting her from her sass as usual.

Mike dropped his head so his forehead rested on Kate's and he could stare into her eyes. Did she realize that she was at the core of this? It was her that had made it possible. Meeting her and falling in love that long-ago summer had shaped his life. Her acceptance of his desires and those of his best friends had brought them to this place where they could be honest about what they needed and how their rapture triggered each other's.

He loved her and the life she'd given him. The children who made him laugh, and sometimes want to pull out his hair. It was all because of her.

"I love you," he murmured as he began to rock, impaling her on his cock a little more gently than he might have otherwise.

He should have known she wasn't going to settle for only some of him.

Kate bit his lower lip, then ordered, "Fuck me, Mike. Like you know I want it."

He couldn't have stopped then if he'd wanted to. He dug his knees into the carpet and adjusted his weight so that he pressed more fully into her, his elbows bearing the brunt of his force where he levered himself above her.

Kate purred and rubbed up against him, as if it turned her on even more when her chest caressed his. Hell, maybe it did. So he shifted his hand from her hair to her breast and flicked his thumb over the hardened peak of her nipple. It wasn't usually her most erogenous zone, but he remembered clearly that when she'd been pregnant before, her body had responded in all sorts of ways it didn't ordinarily.

It seemed this was one.

Kate's pussy fisted around his cock, making it more difficult for him to fuse himself as tightly to her unless he went faster, and drilled harder into her. When he glanced to his right, he saw Joe was matching him stroke for stroke as he fucked Morgan.

They were lost in their own rapture and yet caught up in the group's. The crew on the other side of the phone was doing the same, fitted together in a chain as though they would never break apart.

Mike kept thinking over and over, as he filled Kate and listened to the rest of his friends doing the same with their partners, that they could make this work. No matter what came next.

That thought alone made him nearly shoot deep in his wife.

Even if they weren't in the same location, he got an identical—okay, *almost* identical—thrill from knowing they were safe and loved and about to be very sated. Maybe that would mean he could stay to help Joe out for a bit longer. He'd have to talk to them. Call a group meeting this weekend when they were together in Middletown for Kyra, Ollie, and Van's big day.

But for now...he had other things on his mind.

Mike growled, "What's going on over there?"

Of course he could hear the ecstasy in their vocalizations, which he'd come to recognize through the years. But he wanted them to say it out loud. To admit that even like this, it was so damn good.

"James is fucking me," Devon moaned.

The slap of skin on skin grew louder as they picked up the pace. Joe and Mike did the same as they all made love to one beat, as if they were dancing to a song only the crew could hear.

"Neil is fucking me!" James cried out.

"And Dave has his huge cock up my ass." Neil laughed as he said it, enjoying it even if he pretended it was some kind of imposition to be spread around Dave's fat shaft.

"You know you like it." Dave, who was rarely very aggressive, drew a look from Mike. His brow raised, he wondered if being separated might give the others a chance to grow like being here did for Joe, and for him.

It never hurt to try something new. Hell, that was practically their motto. Why should now be any different?

That thought alone had Mike poised on the verge of losing control. He rode Kate, his hands migrating to her hips to anchor her in place as he gave her what she had asked for and so desperately needed. In sync with each other, it would only take one of them to cave before their partner and the rest of the crew followed right behind.

Joe whipped his gaze to Mike and said, "I hope you're not planning on dragging this out. I..."

"What?" Mike asked through gritted teeth.

"I missed you guys." Joe tipped his head back, the tendons in his neck standing out as he grappled with his self-control. "This. I missed *this*."

"Me too," Morgan cooed as she caressed his cheek.

"Thought that time up at the cabin might have been our last," Dave groaned.

"It wasn't. It wasn't," Devon chanted as if to reassure herself and both of her husbands, who moaned in response. "We're still a crew. We're still together, even if we're...not."

"Then prove it," Mike commanded. "The crew that fucks together comes together. Who's ready?"

A chorus of agreements and moans was exactly what he needed.

"Good, because I can't hold on any longer. Not with you here, sharing this moment with us." Mike roared, then let go. He felt Kate squeeze around him, her pussy rippling along his length as he took off and flew. "Now. Do it now."

Joe jerked beside him as Morgan and Kate screamed out their releases.

The phone crackled as the crew's cries distorted over the speaker. Their unmistakable bliss caused his balls to draw up tight to his body as he poured his release into Kate. And as they rode out the storm of ecstasy together, they kissed, touching each other everywhere while his rocking subsided and their heart rates began to slow to something that wouldn't require immediate medical attention.

Mike sighed and rolled off Kate, lying beside her next to Morgan and Joe. He didn't want to crush her, especially now. Morgan kissed his shoulder and ruffled his hair. Joe clapped him on the back. "Congratulations, you guys. You know we're here for you if you need anything."

Devon echoed their sentiments. "Absolutely. Joe's got your back when you're up there and we'll do the same when you're home. I know you're probably freaking out about being pregnant without Morgan, Kate. And I know I'm no expert when it comes to tiny humans, but I hope you know Kayla and I will do our best to help out."

Kate relaxed fully then, going limp on the sunny carpet beside Mike. She knuckled the corner of her eye and sniffled, making Mike hug her even tighter to him. "Thanks, Devon. All of you. I appreciate that. I'm not going to lie, I am a little worried. I'm older now and...yeah. You're right, but we stick together. And with you, we're in good hands. Thank you."

Steering things to lighter territory, and also to maintain the balance he considered himself in charge of in the group, Mike turned to the crew on the camera, intentionally meeting Dave's gaze as he flopped on his back, sandwiching Neil and James between him and Devon. "You're going to have to make this up to Kayla. Maybe call back much later tonight."

"Don't worry, I will. *We* will. We'll let her be the center of attention tonight."

Kate teased, "Just make sure you lock the door. Abby and Landry don't always remember to knock."

"You know we'll take good care of them," Dave promised. "Besides, we gave them walkie talkies so they can call over to the main house if they need anything… you know, like a restock of the s'mores ingredients and sodas Kayla hooked them up with."

"Oh God, they're going to be on a sugar high for the next year." Morgan shook her head, but she was smiling when she said it.

For a few moments they were silent, with huge smiles on their faces. Mike figured the rest of the crew was as relieved as him to see they could find ways to keep connected, no matter the circumstances.

"Welp, some of us don't get to lounge around all day." Devon cracked her knuckles, then started getting dressed. "Our break is long over. We've got work to do. A ton of it."

Mike winced; he hadn't even asked. "How's the project going? Is everything okay?"

"Yup, fine. Totally fine." James had always been a shit liar.

Neil erased the unease that threatened to coalesce in Mike's gut when he added, "It's under control. We'll get this done. Don't worry about us. Take care of things out there with Joe and we'll do the same here."

"If you need something, you'll call, right?" Mike peered into the phone until the rest of the crew nodded. Even Dave, though as he crossed his arms over his mammoth chest, Mike found it hard to believe there was anything they couldn't handle on their own.

They probably didn't need him as much as he liked to think.

"Congratulations again, see you this weekend." Dave waved, the others mimicked him, then he disconnected.

For a while, the four of them stretched out together in the sunshine beaming in the windows like contented cats. Mike contemplated passing out for a solid afternoon nap when the doorbell began ringing like there was a contest for who could press it the most number of times in ten seconds. Then he heard Nathan, Joe's son, shouting, "Hey, Dad! I know you're in there. When am I going to be old enough for my own key? I proved I can take care of a puppy, so I'm pretty sure I deserve one."

The four of them scrambled to put on their clothes like teenagers getting busted by their parents, instead of the other way around. Their naughty bits were covered, if haphazardly, in seconds flat.

Joe looked around and got the all clear from the rest of them before jogging toward the front door. When he opened it, Gavyn—the owner of the Hot Rides motorcycle shop, the sister garage to Hot Rods—was standing there grinning.

He had Joe's kids and was clearly dropping them off on his way back to Hot Rides.

"Figured since you and Amber have a baby in the house, everyone else should be interrupted too?" Joe grumbled even as he opened his arms to his children with a grin. Gavyn and Amber's infant son, Noah, was the latest addition to the Hot Rides gang. Though not for long as Eli, Alanso, and Sally's baby, plus now Mike and Kate's too —damn, it still didn't seem real—were about to follow right behind them.

Hell, they should kick in together for some day care options. Or at least they could if he and Kate were hanging around like Joe and Morgan. Why had Mike started thinking that way?

"Hey, you were here for hours. I figured you'd be worn out by now." Gavyn stepped inside and hugged Kate, then held his fist out toward Mike, who bumped it. "Congratulations, by the way."

"Thanks," Mike's heart warmed all over as it started to sink in that this was really happening.

As everyone mingled, Nathan and Klea were in a rush to tell Morgan, Joe, Kate, and Mike about the cool things they'd done over at Hot Rods that day. Their puppy echoed their enthusiasm, hopping and nipping at Mike's pants. In that moment, all he could think of was how happy Abby would be if she were there to go on adventures with her best buddy Nathan every day.

He stared out the window as he was surrounded by both old and new friends, *family*, and thought about the future.

When he glanced back, Kate had her hand on her abdomen and was smiling softly at him. She seemed different than when she'd first arrived in Middletown, now serene and at ease where before she'd been frantic and exhausted. There was something about this place. Joe smiled as he looked between Mike and Kate, reaching out to hold Morgan's hand.

Kate nodded, then mouthed, *I love you.*

And Mike knew that no matter what came next, they were in it together.

That was the only thing that mattered.

9
____

A few days after arriving in Middletown, Kate was chatting with Morgan as she walked into Joy, Walker, and Dane's house at Hot Rides. Caught up in their conversation, she didn't notice the place had been strewn with blue and pink streamers and balloons until someone yelled, "SURPRISE!"

She stopped short, causing Morgan to run into her back. Everyone inside cracked up.

"What?" Kate's hands flew to her cheeks. "What is this?"

The stork decorations and women with beaming faces surrounding a mountain of gifts, cake, and punch made it pretty clear what was going on, but she couldn't believe they would do this for her. It was a tight squeeze to jam so many friends in the two-bedroom tiny home, which made it seem like it was bursting at the seams with positivity and well wishes. Suddenly Kate felt a wash of heat spread across her face.

"It's your baby shower!" Joy rushed over, her infant daughter Arden riding her hip. "I know it's really early still, but you're here and it's been a while since your kids were little, and Amber and I have so much our babies are already growing out of...and you're going home soon, sooooooooo...we didn't want to miss out on our chance to tell you how happy we are for you and help you out."

"You guys, this is so sweet." Kate sniffled, wanting to blame her emotions on pregnancy hormones instead of the tumultuous feelings that had been rioting inside her lately. Concerns about their future, envy that Morgan and Joe were embarking on this new adventure in Middletown, aspirations for her own antique business, which could expand exponentially someplace like this. And now a new baby. It was a lot. "Thank you. Really."

She opened her arms and was immediately surrounded by people who cared about her, including Ms. Brown, who was one of the first to embrace her and offer her congratulations once again. This time more eloquently, now that Kate hadn't just shocked the hell out of them all, herself and her husband included.

Amber, Ms. Brown's oldest daughter, followed behind her mom. She rocked Noah, her and Gavyn's son, in the crook of one arm like a pro. Would Kate remember how to do that? Would it be like riding a bike and come rushing back the instant she was handed her newest child?

Things had changed since Landry was a baby. Safety regulations were different, nutritional guidelines, everything. She was going to have to learn all over again. But for the first time since she'd faced doing this without Morgan by her side, she felt like there were people she could lean on, ask questions of, and rely on. Remembering this moment during sleepless nights would go a long way toward calming her anxieties.

Kate peeked at baby Noah and Arden, and the urge to

snuggle them and keep them safe was so strong, she knew no matter what it took, she would give her baby the best life possible. As she looked around the room, and thought of Middletown beyond those four walls, she wondered for a moment if that might mean being as brave as Joe and Morgan had been, starting out fresh here with greater opportunities.

Sometime soon, she was going to have to get her thoughts in order and talk through them with Mike. But not right then. Right then she simply wanted to enjoy an afternoon of celebration. They played games, ate enough for three days, and mingled, people coming and going in small groups where everyone—from the motorcycle mechanics to the Hot Rods' wives to her and Morgan— miraculously found something in common, even if it was their penchant for polyamory.

Kate realized that was another thing she loved about coming out there. It wasn't only her and her eight best friends against the world, but there was a whole community of like-minded people there who understood her relationship even if they weren't directly a part of it. People who would listen to problems and give unbiased feedback without belonging to the inner circle. That was something she'd never experienced before. Sure, they talked online and exchanged emails periodically, but this was different.

It made her feel accepted and understood. Like she was normal instead of always having to hide who exactly she loved beyond her husband. There was a freedom in that. One that she didn't take for granted. Even Ms. Brown, who had a traditional relationship with Joe's uncle Tom, was willing to give advice and open to the life her younger daughter Nola lived with one of the Hot Rods mechanics. It was like having a mom and dad again. Ones who doled out unconditional love. Who wouldn't want that?

Kate smiled and sighed softly as she leaned up against the kitchen counter. Joy turned from where she was chopping up some more fruit for the punchbowl and said, "Everything okay?"

"Perfect." Kate went over and hugged her. "Thanks again for hosting. This was really so kind of you. We haven't known each other long, so I really appreciate you thinking of me."

"Honestly, I kind of am living vicariously through you." Joy smiled sadly. "I hid my pregnancy as long as I could, and when I finally had Arden, I was alone except for a midwife. I hope you don't mind, but it's a way for me to pretend I didn't miss out on so much."

Kate squeezed her harder. "Of course not. I'm so sorry you had to go through that. Here I was moping because I wouldn't have my best friend with me during my pregnancy and you did it alone. I'm a cow."

"No, you're the smart one. I'm a weirdo." Joy shrugged. "I'm okay with that most of the time, but I admit, that stung. Although keeping Arden to myself meant I didn't have to share her either, which is a bit selfish. I guess that makes me a cow too."

Kate didn't know the details of how she, Walker, and Dane had wound up in Middletown, but she knew it hadn't been a joy ride to get there. She asked, "You're not from here, are you?"

"I only wish I was." Joy deposited the fruit into the punch bowl, washed her hands, then traced her daughter's eyebrow with the tip of her index finger. "This is a perfect place for Arden to grow up. None of the bullshit I dealt with is going to find her here."

Kate nodded. Rumor had it they were on the run from the notorious Wildfire outlaw motorcycle gang. "I'm sorry. I heard a little about your troubles."

"That's a polite way of putting it." Joy laughed. "It's nice of you to say that, though. I've never felt as safe as I do with Walker and Dane. They would kill anyone who tried to hurt Arden like my father hurt us. Hell, everyone here looks after her. It's a great place to raise a child. You know, if you decide you don't want to give up your best friend after all."

Joy looked down at Arden but glanced in Kate's direction from beneath her lashes.

Kate hummed since her own thoughts had wandered in that direction too. "It's got to be a good feeling knowing there are so many people you can count on if you need them." She thought of Joe and his cousin Eli and understood how their connection could be alluring enough to entice Joe to leave the Powertools behind. She hadn't truly gotten it at first, but it was becoming clearer the longer she stayed in Middletown, surrounded by all of these amazing people.

"You know, there's always room for more here." Ms. Brown had ears like an owl. She must have sensed they were talking about serious stuff and came to join them. Though she didn't look directly at Kate, the intense focus she trained on scooping out another cup of punch was a dead giveaway that her comment wasn't nearly as casual as she made it sound.

"Oh no, I mean, our place is back home, not here." The instinctive denial rushed from Kate. She regretted it when Morgan looked up and frowned. Besides, if it was true, why was she thinking of Joe and Morgan's pretty house and the plots of land they'd shown Mike where Uncle Tom had said he could build one just like it? One that would be their own.

She looked out the window at the other tiny homes, cute as a picture from a magazine, which ringed a central fire pit and gathering space. The Hot Rides had what the crew had, and then maybe a little bit more. They lived together in addition to working together, something Kate had often dreamed about.

Kyra joined Ms. Brown at the punch bowl. She must have picked up on their chatter as she approached.

"I bet you and Ollie would get along great and could even go picking together. He focuses on automotive parts, of course, but there's got to be plenty of other treasures for you to find for your antique business if you ride along with him." She smiled as she thought of one of the men she was going to marry that weekend. "He's going on a run Thursday. It's only a few hours away, and I can't go with him since I still have a million last-minute wedding things to take care of, but I'm sure he'd love it if you rode along instead."

Morgan looked over and nodded. "You should do that. Just see how it feels."

Kate bit her lip. "Yeah. I would like that. Thank you. All of you."

She knuckled the corner of her eye before she could start bawling and ruin the lovely party they'd set up for her. Ms. Brown patted her arm, then gave her some space to mull everything over.

Kate watched as Morgan blended in with the women there, who supported and loved each other and the Powertools by association. The crew had been her rock for so long, but what if their circle could expand to include the rest of their acquaintances too?

And not from two states away, but in real and meaningful everyday relationships?

Would it be worth it if she had to give up half of the crew to make it happen? She simply couldn't imagine doing that. Devon, Kayla, Dave, James, and Neil were more than just friends to her. They were lovers. They were confidants. And they needed her.

So why the hell was she feeling panicky and a little sick at the thought of getting in the car at the end of the week and saying goodbye to everyone—including her best friend—she loved in Middletown?

What if she and Mike gave up this opportunity and it never came around again?

Kate put her hand on her stomach and asked her unborn child, "What's best for you? What should we be doing?"

Unfortunately, the baby didn't know how to talk yet.

10

Mike sat at a picnic table under the pavilion covering the barbeque area at the Hot Rods complex. Joe was across from him, reviewing their blueprints and making notes for the ten millionth time in the past half hour. His journal was already more than half-full of scribbles and underlines and arrows and stars with circles around them.

"Dude, you have it worked out. You're good, I swear. Look it's two hours past quitting time on a Friday. You're going to have to take the weekend off or you'll offend the bride and her husbands-to-be, you know?" Mike put his hand over the papers, physically blocking his best friend's line of sight. The rest of the crew should be rolling into town any moment, and when they did, the focus had to be on family. The people they did all of this for.

"I want to make sure the change requests didn't have any unintended consequences." Joe grumbled. "I learned how to do this from you, so if I'm a pain in the ass..."

"You're also freaked out by the accident. I get that." Mike lifted his hand and held it up in front of him, parallel to his chest. "But you know that wasn't your fault, right?"

"It's never happened on a Powertools site where you're in charge."

"Luck has as much to do with that as skill or preparation. At least on my part. You guys and Devon are experienced. You know what you're doing and we've worked together for a really long time. It's hardly the same thing." Mike rubbed the back of his neck. "I've had plenty of nightmares about some close calls we've had. Remember when Neil kept installing shingles despite thunder booming around us to try to beat the coming storm and protect the interior work we'd done on the Malone project? You know, the time he damn near got fried by the lightning that struck the weathervane not ten feet from him?"

"Oh yeah." Joe glanced over to the side as if recalling the incident. "I guess I forgot about that."

"Well, I didn't. It'd be pretty hard to when you're the one responsible. That blue-white zigzag and his smoking boots are permanently embossed on the inside of my eyelids." Mike scrubbed his hand over his face as if he could wipe it away when even the several years in between hadn't been able to erase it.

"You're meant for this. I...I'm not sure I am no matter how much I'd like to be." Joe closed his notebook and put his pen too carefully on top.

"You are." Mike cleared his throat and tested out an idea he'd been mulling over since he'd arrived in Middletown earlier that week. "Maybe the whole crew is."

"Huh?" Joe tipped his head.

"We're not getting any younger." Mike winced. A baby at his age was going to be a whole new challenge. Maybe it was dumb to take on more, but seeing what Joe had been doing here... "What you're working on. It's inspiring me."

"Are you kidding? It's kind of a shit show."

"Only because you're used to being on a high-performing team and this is new. Fresh. And you haven't figured out your process yet. It's going to get better every day...and every project."

"What do you mean? This is a one-time show, remember?" Joe looked at him like he'd hit his head. "I'm out here to expand Hot Rods for Eli and then, well... Then I have no fucking idea what I'm going to do."

"Let's be honest; you're not coming home. This is where you belong. Where your heart wants to stay." Mike voiced his biggest fear out loud. Or what had been his greatest worry. Now he wasn't sure if it might not be the best opportunity they'd had in years.

"It's not like that, Mike. I want two things and I can't have both. How the hell am I supposed to choose?" Joe wrenched his head to the side and stared into the gorgeous greenery around them as if he couldn't bear to meet Mike's gaze. "I've done one for a long ass time. And now it seems like maybe I should do the other, at least for a while, while I have the chance."

"I'm not criticizing you. I don't blame you one bit. It's gorgeous here. And, like I said, there's a lot of potential... for more." Mike cleared his throat. "You're absolutely right. We've had a good, long run. And we can't keep swinging hammers forever. My back is shit and Dave's leg isn't going to hold out much longer."

Joe cursed under his breath.

"But there's no reason we can't graduate from grunt work and do what you're doing. We could expand the business. Here in Middletown, there's plenty of room to grow."

Joe opened his mouth, then closed it. Then opened it again. But whatever he'd been about to say was lost when his son whooped and sprinted past them.

"Uncle Mike! Look!" Nathan shouted as he chucked a chewed-up tennis ball a pretty solid way across the clearing in the woods. His puppy tore after it as if it was the most amazing prize in the world, its floppy ears bouncing as it raced toward the fluorescent-green bit of heaven.

"Good throw, kid!" Mike couldn't wait for his son and daughter to arrive. And to meet their new baby. It hadn't quite sunk in, but he honestly couldn't say he'd ever been happier. Lately things had seemed to be going by too fast. His kids were getting older. Abby especially was on the verge of being too grown for father-daughter shit. It wasn't that he wanted to replace them, but... "Joe, I gotta tell you..."

"Hmm?" His best friend whipped back around, instantly keying in to Mike's serious tone.

"I've been jealous of you lately." There. He'd fucking admitted it.

"Me? What the hell?" Joe cocked his head.

"You've been out here, working on this project. It's bigger than us. Something exciting and new and..."

"Completely out of my league. Don't fucking remind me." Joe groaned.

"It doesn't have to be. What if our game was to change?" Hell, Mike's whole world was about to be different, why not this too?"

"What are you saying? You're not talking about

bringing our regular crew out here to work on this, are you?"

"Not exactly. Like I said, we're getting older. How much longer can we keep going like we are?" Mike frowned.

"I don't know, but that's why we're careful and we've saved..."

"But what if stepping back from construction at some point didn't have to be the end of our careers, but only the beginning?" Mike leaned forward. "Each of us is plenty capable of running a crew. And in a town like this, there's probably enough business to support us without having to compete. Maybe our crew should learn to manage projects instead of doing the work ourselves. Imagine if we had multiple large-scale jobs going on at once? Sure, we might give up some profitability since we would need to add payroll for workers, but with bigger bids like this, I bet we'd still have more than six times the cash coming in. And if we're all foremen, and forewomen, then we could collaborate on this stuff so no one would be going at it alone."

"Wow. That's..." Joe blinked a few times. "I like it. I mean, *really* like it."

"Me too." Mike took a deep, shaky breath. "The only thing holding us back, I think, is Bare Natural. We can't ask Kayla to walk away from her whole business. Her whole life. Everything she and Dave have built there from the ground up. How could we expect her to sacrifice that? And if we can't, how can we pull this concept off when split up? And worse, how could we abandon the pair of them, leaving them behind while we move on."

"You're right," Joe's face fell. "It's not fair to do that to them."

Mike scrubbed his hand over his face. He was probably a fucking traitor to even consider it. But he'd been longing for more. A greater purpose. And to be honest, when Joe had come out to Middletown, Mike had seen the potential, but without a way to reach it.

"If nothing else, *you* should consider it." He tapped his hand on Joe's notebook. "You're ready, whether you believe it or not. Even if it means you leave the rest of us in your dust. You were right. This place is doing wonders for you and for your family."

Joe looked over at Nathan playing tug of war with the puppy over his tennis ball, laughing and rolling around in the grass. He smiled and sighed. "Thanks for saying that. And I'm sure it could be good for you too, except I know you're too decent to abandon the crew, like I did."

Mike would have argued, but just then someone honked the horn from the Hot Rods parking lot almost as furiously as Nathan had rung Joe's doorbell the other day.

The crew! They had arrived.

Mike shot to his feet, a bit guilty maybe, as if they could have overheard what he'd been discussing with Joe. Nathan whizzed past, even more excited to see Abby than he'd been to show off his arm and his dog. Klea was jumping up and down on the porch of Tom and Ms. Brown's cabin, where she'd been helping to make favors for the weekend wedding.

Mike felt at least as eager as the kids to see the rest of the crew and to try to act like things were back to normal. Unfortunately, more than ever he had a feeling they were on a path that couldn't take them home again. At least not together and not the way they'd been for years.

"We'll talk more about this later, okay?" Mike put a hand on Joe's shoulder and clasped it tight. "For the record, I think you just might be the smartest motherfucker I know."

"Can I get that in writing?" Joe flashed his lopsided smile then. "There's lots to think about, I guess. Yeah, we should definitely circle back to this. Some better time."

Mike hoped that didn't mean never. If they waited for everything to be perfect, it would probably never happen. And with every day he spent there, with Joe, in Middletown, he was starting to believe that if he didn't follow his dream, he might regret it for the rest of his life.

With that, they watched as Nathan charged across the lawn, his puppy close on his heels. Abby was running in his direction too. Nathan might have been a couple months younger than her, but he was growing by the day. So when he collided with Abby, he easily scooped her up and swung her around, looking entirely too grown up and too happy to see a girl for either Mike or Joe to be comfortable with.

"We better go chaperone," Mike grumbled. "I don't want to have a kid and a grandkid in the same class at school."

Joe burst out laughing, until he realized that wasn't exactly impossible. "Let's go."

11

Mr. Prickles, the hedgehog, trotted between the rows of guests toward a treat that Ollie dangled from his fingers where he crouched at the head of the aisle. He'd been training his beloved pet for this moment for months. Of course, Mr. Prickles chose that exact moment to hesitate, halfway to his goal, and take a pretty impressive dump.

Good thing the ceremony was outside. Trevon quickly followed behind and scooped the poop while everyone in attendance—especially the kids—cracked up. Mike leaned out into the aisle to snap a picture of Ollie's horrified face with Van, his soon-to-be husband, in the background trying to stifle his own grin behind his hand. It was the perfect way to cut the tension in the group of usually laidback and ultra-familiar friends.

The guys looked sharp but not completely unrecognizable in the black jeans and coordinating sport coats they'd chosen for their big day. The one where they would commit to the woman they shared. Ollie had paired his outfit with a pair of funky black-and-white sneakers while Van wore glossy black boots that made it clear he could kick just about anyone's ass if he so chose. They stood shoulder to shoulder, grasping for each other's hands when the acoustic guitar music being played by one of Kyra's band members changed and the bride appeared from where she'd been waiting at the edge of the woods.

Though Kyra was a badass drummer for Kason Cox's band, she seemed more like a woodland sprite when she materialized from the lush greenery wearing an ethereal dress in muted blush tones.

Mike had no idea what you called the kind of material it was made of, but the way it floated around her on the gentle breeze was downright magical. Especially when paired with the crown of wildflowers she wore and those she carried while Tom walked her up the de-pooped aisle to her fiancés. Wren, the Hot Rides' welder, stood off to the side holding Mr. Prickles so he could witness his people making things official. After all, living in the campervan with them as they toured the country, he'd watched just about every other part of their relationship as it unfolded.

Mike could see why they'd decided to turn their original engagement party date into a full-blown, if modest wedding. He wouldn't have wanted to wait a whole extra year to be joined with his soul mates simply to have some fancy party afterward.

Kate sighed so dramatically Mike thought she might pass out. When he looked over at her she smiled back, her eyes a bit teary. He couldn't help but lean in for a quick kiss before taking her hand in his and turning his attention to the ceremony. He shushed Abby and Nathan, who whispered conspiratorially about the mushy vibe from the row in front of them.

Thankfully, the wedding wasn't very long, but it didn't have to be in order to be profound.

Relationships like theirs—Kyra, Ollie, and Van's, as well as those of most of the people in attendance—defied traditional ceremonies and recognition, so they kept only the stuff that spoke to their hearts and validated the love the three people standing in a triangle before their friends and extended family to share a part of their souls for everyone to see.

And when it was done, sealed with one hell of a three-way kiss, Wren handed Mr. Prickles to Ollie so the trio could head off for some pictures and a moment to gather themselves before returning for the reception. Mike would be shocked if there wasn't some making out involved too. At least there had been on his wedding day with Kate, which he couldn't help but relive every time they were lucky to share a similarly sacred moment with their friends and family.

While the guests of honor were gone, the Hot Rides guys transformed the clearing, rearranging the chairs and setting up tables laden with about a billion candles for the dinner that Devra had prepared along with help—and a big-ass cake—from Morgan. Mike tried to help but was assured it was under control.

"Dad, can we go play with Nathan, Klea, and the rest of the kids?" Landry asked.

"Of course." Mike stroked his hair, loving that for a little while longer he leaned into the touch instead of dodging it. "Just don't go too far into the woods and make sure you eat something decent before you dig into the desserts, okay?"

"I'll watch him, Dad." Abby looked over her shoulder, already angling toward Nathan, where he held his puppy, who was sporting a navy blue bowtie, on a leash. "Come on, Landry."

"Thanks, Abby." Mike wished he could hug her, but she was officially past the stage for public affection.

Kate had gone off to assist Morgan with last-minute details and who knew what else, so Mike wandered over to Joe, who stood by Eli, Uncle Tom, and a couple of the Hot Rods and Hot Rides guys. One by one the rest of the crew trickled over too, expanding the circle of friends more and more. They'd been shooting the shit for a while when Kason ambled in their direction, his arm slung around some guy's shoulder. He should be careful or his husband and wife—Wren and Jordan—were going to get jealous. Kason was the lead singer of the country band that Kyra played drums for. Both Kyra's new husband, Van, and Kason's husband, Jordan, managed security for the group when they were on tour. At least when Jordan wasn't also working on "security" matters for other private businesses and gray areas of the government.

Mike didn't know all the details, and sure as hell was smarter than to ask.

Kason, however, knew everyone. Or at least lots of people with more money than Mike would ever dream of making in his lifetime. So when he steered this guest right between Mike and Joe, it was pretty obvious it wasn't for a casual introduction to a friend-of-a-friend-of-a-friend.

"These are the guys I was telling you about," Kason said to his buddy before lifting his chin in Mike's direction. "This is Mike, the foreman of the Powertools crew, and Joe, who's heading up the renovations and new build at Hot Rods that you were drooling over. Guys, this is Giovanni, a buddy of mine who's retiring from the entertainment business with a whole lot of capital and some ideas for something to keep him busy in his old age."

"It's a pleasure. Nice to meet people who actually work for a living instead of standing on a stage and collecting panties and briefs, like this asshole." The guy laughed and then stuck out his hand. "And if it doesn't make me as bad as him, talking about work at a party like this, I'd love to hear what you think of my plans and see if maybe you think a crew like yours could pull them off."

Mike looked at Joe and raised a brow while Dave nudged him in the ribs. He wasn't going to assume the lead, not here, not when Joe was establishing himself in a new role, and not when he'd been trying to tell his best friend that chances like this were right under their noses here in Middletown.

Joe shrugged one shoulder. "I'm always interested in big ideas and helping bring them to life."

Mike tried not to break out into a shit-eating grin as Dave threw in a good word for his buddy too. It was then he realized that no matter what it meant for each of them personally, they wanted the best for each other. And even the others could see, this had the potential to be a big deal for Joe.

But what about the rest of them? Could it work for them too?

"I'm thinking of building something kind of outrageous. I mean, I might be leaving show business, but it'll never leave my blood." He crossed his arms. "A tattoo shop. Not the hole-in-the-wall kind. The sort we see out in L.A. A destination studio. Middletown is big enough, plus with all the resorts around, who wouldn't want to book a spot and stay for a weekend getaway? Plus, well, I'm hoping to lure my daughter—who's a pretty popular artist—out here to the middle of fucking nowhere, as she likes to call it, with me. So the flashier the better, you know?"

"Joe did the designs for Hot Rods himself. He's focusing on our living quarters first since my wife is pregnant, but you should see what he has drawn up for a garage upgrade and retail space addition." Eli clapped Joe on the shoulder, and Mike could have kissed him. "He can definitely hook you up. Hell, your shop might even be a good tie in with the folks that come out here because of our reality show. Seems like it might be the same crowd."

"You're right." Giovanni leaned in, not at all casual anymore. "Do you have a portfolio you could show me? Or maybe I could hire you for a mock-up? When is the soonest your crew is available given that they're all-in on Hot Rods right now?"

Joe hesitated, but Mike subtly knocked his boot into his friend's and Joe squared his shoulders. "Hot Rods is my first official project on my own. It's something I've been mulling over for a while but never really got the chance to try my hand at until Eli told me what he was envisioning and couldn't find anywhere else. So what you've seen at Hot Rods is pretty much my entire portfolio, but we could set up a time to meet and I could do some sketches for you. We could see where it goes from there, if you want."

Mike hadn't realized Joe was interested in pursuing design. Why hadn't he said anything? Maybe because he didn't have time to chase his dreams when he was obligated to working with the Powertools day in and day out. He glanced around at the rest of his crew, and Neil whipped his gaze away. He'd known! But he hadn't spilled either. The crew didn't do secrets. Things would fall apart if they did. Had it already been starting without him realizing it?

Shit, maybe it really was time to rethink things. What else had Mike missed while he was so busy trying to maintain the status quo? What about Neil, James, Devon, and Dave? Were they putting aside aspirations or being held back by being grunts all these years? And what would they do as they got older when swinging a hammer, crawling over roofs, and hauling heavy loads no longer suited them as well?

The problem was that back home, they didn't have access to a market like they would in Middletown, which was easily ten times as large. But the rest of the crew had roots there, and Joe had them here. How could they get past that? Maybe they couldn't, but Mike's vision could become Joe's reality. He'd be glad to help the guy every step along the way to make it come to life if that's what he wanted too.

"Well, it looks like the happy throuple is about to make their entrance, but here's my card. Give me a call next week and we can set something up." Giovanni passed his info to Joe.

"Thank you. I will do that. It was great to meet you." Joe tucked it into his pocket then patted the fabric over it as if to make sure it was safe.

"Same goes. Enjoy the party." Giovanni wandered off toward his gorgeous and much-younger date.

Kason knocked his shoulder into Joe's. "So...what do you think? Would you like to stick around for more than the summer? I know Eli and Tom love having you here."

"We do." Eli looked like he was holding his breath.

Truth be told, so was Mike.

Joe stammered, "Uh, I don't know. We've been so caught up in making right now work that we haven't made any decisions about the future yet. Things are going great with Morgan and Devra. Morgan showed me a real estate listing for the empty storefront next to the restaurant where she could expand either temporarily, more long term, or with some sort of franchise-type situation. If I can get it together with the construction stuff...it seems like I might be dumb to ignore what's right in front of me. Nothing is written in stone yet, just...possibilities. I guess I need to talk to Morgan some more. Seriously, though, thank you for that. It means a lot."

"No trouble at all. You guys really are amazing at what you do. I've seen what you've built here at Hot Rides and the draft you gave Kyra, Ollie, and Van for something a bit bigger and more permanent than their campervan, which, by the way, I've told them I'd like to pay for as a wedding gift. Besides, your work at Hot Rods makes me think I might need to do some renovations at my own place. Maybe a serious upgrade to our old fishing cabin on the waterfront. You know people would be lining up to sign with you and the rest of your crew if you moved out here and decided you wanted the work."

"You going to keep bringing your rich friends over?" Mike joked.

"I mean, I didn't want to irritate you, but there are three other people who are interested in development work in the area after coming to hang out at the lodge with us over the past year. People fall in love with Middletown. I'm telling you I know a thousand Giovannis if you're interested in that kind of stuff. Just let me know." Kason shrugged as if it was nothing. As if he hadn't connected the dots between the vision Mike had been nearly too afraid to put out there between him and Joe the other day and something that could actually happen.

Well, shit.

Now that he knew what was possible, Mike couldn't unknow it. Would he be able to walk away? And even if he could, would it be the right thing to do? Would he be happy going back to the crew if he was positive he was stifling their careers?

Mike only knew one thing for sure: they were going to need to have a crew meeting soon. One with actual, serious discussions and their clothes on.

But not before they had a chance to continue this party in private. It had been too long since they'd been together, and they needed each other. Needed to feel part of the thing that had defined them for so long, even if it might not do so in the future.

12

Mike's patience had just about run out. Was he glad to have the whole crew there, partying with the Hot Rods and Hot Rides gangs? Of course. Was he full of excellent food and one of the best cakes Morgan had ever made? Oh yeah.

But was he still hungry? Hell fucking yes.

Given everything that had happened lately and his own wayward thoughts about how Joe maybe had the right idea about moving to Middletown, he desperately needed some alone time with his crew to nail them back together again. Literally.

Kate must have seen the hunger in his eyes from across the room. She hugged Ms. Brown, then headed in his direction with a sultry smile. "All the kids are going with Tom and Ms. Brown to Kason's house. He promised them they could have a sleepover in tents on the beach beside his indoor pool. I thought Landry might be a little uncomfortable spending the night somewhere new without us, but nope...he was first in the Hot Rods' bus to head over there, sandwiched in between Sabra and Holden's twins. Barely waved goodbye."

Mike didn't blame him. The country megastar's hillside retreat was enough to make anyone envious. The indoor oasis was damn near a waterpark. Maybe sometime he'd have to arrange for the crew to have an overnighter there, while the kids stayed back at Hot Rods.

His imagination went wild with possibilities.

Or maybe that was his libido.

Either way, he was about to call an end to these festivities so they could begin others. It seemed like the Hot Rods and Hot Rides groups were having similar thoughts. The regular guests had excused themselves hours ago, and now it was down to just them. Where they'd mingled seamlessly earlier, they began to sort themselves out and mill around in three distinct clumps.

Quinn, Mike, and Eli gathered at the center. Each of them the unofficial head of their clan.

"Time to split up?" Quinn asked, glancing over his shoulder at his husband, Trevon, who was slow dancing with their wife, Devra.

"Yup." Eli grinned as he stared over at his wife, Sally, who was sitting in their husband Alanso's lap, her hands folded on her not-so-flat stomach. "I want to take full advantage of the romantic mood while Sally's still up for it. This might have to last us a few months."

Mike snorted. "With an infant in the house, you're going to be lucky to find the energy for a year."

"Then it sounds like you better make the best of tonight too," Quinn teased.

And it hit Mike all over again. Yeah. A baby. His. Kate's. They were starting again. Except this time they were going to be older and more tired.

"You're right. Gotta go. Thanks for the food and for including us in the big day. Tell Kyra, Ollie, and Van the same when you can think straight again, will you?" Mike shook Quinn's hand. He was so grown and confident now, compared to the troubled teenager he'd been when they'd first met. Maybe it was knowing he was going to be a dad again, or because no matter how old you were, you sometimes needed someone to tell you when you did something right, but he used his grip to pull Quinn into a one-armed hug and said, "You're doing great, kid. I always knew you'd figure things out. Have fun with your gang tonight."

"Uh, thanks." Quinn ducked his head, the hint of his sheepish, younger self peeking through for just a moment. "That means a lot coming from you."

Eli cut through their sentimental moment with an elbow to Mike's ribs. "You know that goes for you, too. Right?"

Mike felt that sincere question like a punch to the gut. Because lately, no, he didn't. "I don't know, Eli. My crew is split, maybe for good. And suddenly I'm thinking about what it would be like if I followed Joe down this new path he's blazing. What the fuck kind of leader does it make me to think of leaving half my crew behind even for a moment?"

"A human one." Eli put his hand on Mike's shoulder and squeezed. "It's okay to want better for yourself and for all of them. I hope you get a chance to talk about Giovanni's proposal. You know, tomorrow."

"Yeah, tomorrow." Mike sighed, then pushed the heavy thoughts out of his mind in favor of epic distractions. "So... See you all then, but not too early?"

"Brunch sounds good. We'll each bring a dish. Devra

makes these pancake things drizzled in honey that you'll want a million of, especially if you burn as many calories as I know we will." Quinn nodded, then waved as he spun on the heel of his motorcycle boots. "Have a good night."

As if everyone had been waiting for the cue, they echoed Quinn's sentiment, the three groups waving to each other as they dispersed. The Hot Rides walked toward the clearing in the woods where they'd set up a fairytale-worthy gazebo surrounded by mosquito netting filled with dozens of Moroccan lanterns and a mountain of cushions.

The Hot Rods gang took off, their perfectly polished restored cars a parade of sexy vehicles and revving engines. The smallest bunch—the nine Powertools—piled into two vans they'd borrowed from the mechanics' latest venture, an offshoot of the two garages where Ollie directed the conversion of vans into amazing tiny homes on wheels like his own.

Mike drove one and James the other. They stayed together as they made the short trip through the woods to Joe and Morgan's rented house.

Home was where they all were, together. For right then, that was here.

No one talked much, the anticipation building as each couple or trio sat close enough together to get in a few gentle touches and soft words en route. So when they arrived, Mike didn't make any pretense. He waited for Joe to unlock the door, then stepped inside and pointed to the stairs before ushering everyone toward the finished lower level. There was plenty of room down there for what he had in mind.

Without needing to be told, Neil and Dave began stripping the cushions from the mammoth sectional, arranging them on the ground. Kate entered last, having detoured for a few linens, which she held out to Morgan and Kayla. They used fitted sheets to gather and shape the cushions, and before he knew it, they'd transformed the open area into a proper adult play space complete with several faux-mattresses pushed together to make an enormous bed.

Mike stood at the center and held his hand out to Kate, who was there to entwine her fingers with his in an instant. Joe and Morgan, Dave and Kayla, and Neil, James, and Devon fanned out in an arc facing them, waiting for him to give them some direction.

For the first time in a while, he wasn't sure he was the right person to do that. No matter what Eli had said earlier, he felt like an imposter. "So..."

Neil cocked his head. "What the hell is that? This is the part where you ask why we're still wearing clothes and start being bossy as fuck."

"Is that what everyone still wants?" Mike asked. "Or is it time that each of us took more control of our own lives? I used to think I was standing up for each of us and our needs. Am I actually just getting in the way?"

"What?" Kayla, the most sensitive of the group, reached for Mike's free hand. "You can't really believe that."

"Is this because I left?" Joe took a step forward too. "Shit, I'm sorry. That had nothing to do with you, or me wanting to be in charge. I swear. I keep trying to tell you..."

"Words aren't enough." Dave put his hand on Joe's elbow and squeezed, stopping him in his tracks. "We're going to have to drill this into his head."

Devon nodded, grinning at James while she did. "I like the sound of that."

"You'll always be our foreman," James told Mike. "Even if each of us is working with another crew or no crew at all. You're stuck with us."

As if to prove it to him, James started taking his clothes off. As soon as his shirt cleared his head, everyone else followed his example. They began undressing around Mike until he was the only one still decent. That included Kate, who shimmied out of the gorgeous plum satin dress she'd worn to the wedding, then kicked it to one side.

It turned him on even more than her exposed bare skin when she put her hands on her hips and said, "Remind us where we belong."

Mike went from half-hard to fully erect at the steel in her tone and the force of her bravado. She was every bit as churned up as him, he was sure of it, but she put her faith in him, and the crew, to settle that unease. He should be more like Kate.

"Yeah." James aimed a heated glare at Mike, as if he would let them down. "That's what I want most tonight. To know that no matter where we go from here, this is forever. I'm Powertools for life. So get over here and show me it's true. That when I kneel for you, you're going to be there to take what I'm giving. Now and in the future, whatever that looks like."

Mike would have ripped his own clothes off then if Kate wasn't there helping him shed them as quickly as possible. Kayla, Morgan, and Devon joined in, ridding him of his socks, undoing his pants, and shoving down his underwear even as Kate finished peeling off his shirt.

Having four women prepare him to fuck their

husbands was enough to give any man a rush. Mike wasn't strong enough to deny it even if he should.

Neil was whispering something that sounded reassuring to James in between kisses. He glared over his husband's shoulder at Mike as if promising to rip his balls off if he didn't treat James right.

"You know I would never hurt him. Or any of you. Not intentionally, and I swear I'll do my best to do right by you all."

"You have to be included in that." James twisted then, looking over his shoulder as Mike flanked him, sandwiching him against Neil. "You can't take care of us if you don't look after yourself."

"I'm about to do that right now," Mike promised, unable to keep himself restrained even a moment longer. Not when so much of their world had shifted in the past weeks, with Joe moving, Kate getting pregnant, and now him questioning pillars of his life he'd thought were carved in stone for years.

He needed the crew as much, if not more, than they needed him. And he intended to show them just how desperately. It figured that the rest of them were in sync with him.

Dave reached down and grabbed Mike's cock, which hung heavy between his thighs. He slathered it with lube, stroking it a few more times than was entirely necessary for the job. While Dave got Mike ready, Devon took care of James, drizzling lube over her husband's ass and rubbing it in. Neil kept kissing the shit out of James even as Kate crouched beside them for an up-close view, then drew Mike's face to her for a taste of her own.

It was too much. If he intended to follow through on

his plan, to take each one of the guys and ride them until they were mindless with pleasure, he was going to have to get going.

"What are you waiting for?" James asked as he broke from Neil for a moment.

"Nothing." Mike grasped James's hip in one hand and his own cock in the other, then sank into the slighter man. Pure pleasure traveled up his cock, which squeezed between the tight ring of muscles. James groaned and pushed back, taking all of Mike and giving him exactly what he craved.

As he did, Neil was there soothing James, kneading his chest and rubbing his abs, easing the initial discomfort of Mike's intrusion.

Dave and Joe mirrored Neil and James so that the four men knelt in pairs, two side by side and two facing each other with Mike behind James on one side. He planned to make his way around the entire square, if he was strong enough to hold on in the face of so much temptation.

"Fuck, that's hot." Devon moaned and touched herself. "Get them good and worked up, Mike. I can't wait for my guys to fuck me when you've driven them wild."

Neil flashed her a look that promised he wasn't going to go easy on her or disappoint her. Then he reached for James's cock and began to stroke it in time to Mike's unrelenting thrusts. It wouldn't take long, with them both using James roughly, as he preferred, for the other man to hit his limit.

After a few minutes, Mike began to sweat. He wrapped his arm around James's chest and pinned the smaller man to him. He felt the thump of James's heart beneath his palm and couldn't resist biting his neck. James clamped down on Mike's dick, feeling a little too good. Fortunately, that also meant he was close to tapping out.

"If you do that again, I'm going to come." James cursed. "I wanted to go longer."

"Next time," Mike promised him. James didn't often last the longest, but he was able to come the most often of any of the guys. "For now I need you to take care of Devon so I can work on Neil."

"Oh fuck. Let go." James squirmed then, dislodging Mike. They both groaned.

James dove for Devon, tackling her to the cushions. They both giggled as he rolled to his back and lifted her on top of him. He held her hips, helping her align herself. She took his cock in hand and guided it to her pussy, sinking onto it while the seven other people around them licked their lips in anticipation of their own similar joining with their spouses.

Sex with their partner was incredible, but when it was boosted by sharing with the crew, like now, it was mind-blowing. Witnessing the power had Mike strangling the base of his cock to keep from seeking out Kate and ending this game far too early.

While Devon rode James, who gritted his teeth and stared at the ceiling as if begging for an ounce more stamina, Mike spun Neil around. First he reached between the man's legs to cup his balls and tease him as he watched his husband and wife fucking in front of them.

"Come on, Mike." Neil groaned. "I'm not going to last past them coming together."

"I'll go first." Dave shrugged one of his meaty shoulders. "You know, to be nice."

Mike laughed at that. Despite his cock being hard as a

steel spike and the troubling stuff he'd been ruminating on lately, here and now, things were as they should be.

"Very gentlemanly of you," Kayla purred as she approached her husband. She trailed her hand down his cheek and neck, making him shiver and his cock grow even more than it already had. But when her fingers toyed with the piercing in his nipple, his nostrils flared. She knew exactly how to play him.

It wasn't especially difficult, especially with Devon and James's growing moans and the slick slap of their flesh making a soundtrack that echoed around the room.

Dave swallowed hard. "Damn, that looks like it feels so good. Just like it did when you were fucking him."

"It's been a while since we've done this," Mike said as he took his place behind the big guy. Over his shoulder he saw Kate cupping her breast as she watched without blinking. She always loved watching him fuck the crew. And tonight wouldn't be any exception.

Joe noticed Mike's stare and curled his fingers. Both Kate and Morgan came to him, kneeling on either side of him. He reached out stroking them both, one with each hand. What he did to his own wife, he also did to Mike's, making sure she was included and taken care of, even when Mike couldn't do it personally. Kate smiled and kissed Joe before Morgan took a turn.

When Mike watched them, he couldn't hold out any longer. He had to be back inside someone, fucking, and driving home these feelings he'd been terrified he'd lose. Showing them he loved them all, even if he didn't know what was best at the moment.

Mike took hold of his cock and aligned it with Dave's body. Kayla grabbed the back of her husband's neck and devoured him in a fierce kiss as Mike took possession of his ass. He grunted and Kayla devoured it, sucking on his tongue and flicking the stud there the way that drove Dave nuts.

James and Devon were studying their interaction as Devon ground on top of James. They were panting and writhing, a flurry of movement that couldn't be sustained. Neil noticed too and cheered them on. He lunged for the couple and put a hand on each, as if needing to be connected to them when they surrendered to the energy pulsing through the room and each other.

Mike nodded at them. "Go ahead. Come. James, fill her up so Neil can feel you when he gets in there."

James shouted and his hips levered off the ground. Devon's spine arched, her head went back, her small breasts pert and her nipples tight as she screamed and shook. James followed right behind her, pumping into her as he emptied himself deep into her pussy.

Mike shuddered, sinking to the root in Dave's ass. Hot, tight flesh gripped him as he began to ride, inspired by the display Devon and James put on as they gave in to the desire that joined them all.

Morgan was stroking Joe's cock while he had the fingers of one hand buried in Kate and the other in his wife. Whatever he was doing, they seemed to appreciate it. Mike focused, leaning forward until Dave went onto all fours. It was the easiest position for him given his bum leg and the fact that Mike didn't plan to take it easy on him because of an old injury or any other reason.

The guy could handle him.

He picked up the pace, knowing he couldn't last the entire night. Not when surrounded by the people he loved most with emotions running high. But when Dave reached for his cock, Mike growled, "Not yet. Don't touch it or you'll ruin the ending."

He anchored the bigger man's hips and withdrew his rock-hard cock from Dave's ass with a grimace. The cool air on his dick was a rude awakening after being nestled in warm, moist flesh. Mike slapped Dave's ass. "Give it to Kayla. Go ahead."

Dave didn't have to be told twice—he practically smothered his wife, landing with his hips firmly wedged between her long, pale thighs, which were decorated with colorful tattoos. She purred and arched her back, making it easy for him to sink inside her body to find familiar pleasure despite his thick cock.

Neil laughed at Dave's urgency, even if it was a bit raspy.

"You think you could do any better?" Mike slid sideways on the carpet until he was behind Neil instead. "Devon already got off once. You're going to have to work hard to make her come again. You think you can do that after I put you on the edge?"

"I will." Neil stared at his wife, who was curled up on their husband's chest. Her flushed cheeks and bright eyes said she was ready for the challenge.

"I'm always up for seconds," Devon toyed with the slickness between her legs, proof of how well James had flooded her not long before. "Go, Mike. Get him so fucking hard and eager I can't help but come on him when he fucks me."

"You heard her," Neil rasped at Mike. "Do it. Do *me*."

James's cock twitched where it rested, already half-hard again, against their wife's hip. Devon and James kissed, then looked to Mike, waiting for him to put on a show that would rev Devon up in time for Neil to finish her off again.

Joe was doing the same for Morgan and Kate, rubbing their clits with his thumbs as he pumped his long fingers in and out of them. Kate reached over and squeezed Mike's hand. "Hurry."

Mike did as she urged. He aimed the blunt head of his cock at Neil's hole, bouncing it off the tensed muscles there until the other guy moaned and thrust his ass in the air. Then he drizzled more lube over his cock and Neil's hole before he began to work it open.

"Shit." Neil pounded the floor with his fist. "It's been a minute since you fucked me last."

"Too much?" Mike paused, though it damn near killed him not to drill inside and start riding Neil like he knew they both needed. By the time he made it to Joe, he was going to be frantic.

"No." Neil looked over his shoulder. "It'll never be enough. I just didn't think we'd be doing this again...for a while. And now that we are..."

Mike reached around and fisted Neil's cock, rewarding him for being honest while keeping him hard and ready despite the emotional release he obviously needed as much as the physical one.

Joe took a shaky breath, encouraging Morgan and Kate to smother him with hugs. "I'm sorry. I didn't mean to take Mike away from you guys or to tear us apart even more."

Mike growled, then bit Neil's shoulder so he knew that even if Mike wasn't there day to day, that didn't mean he was giving up possession of any of them. "That isn't going to happen. We're a crew for life. Right?"

He scanned the room, and everyone nodded. Mike

wrapped his arms around Neil and lifted, turning the man so he faced Joe with Morgan and Kate on either side of him. "Kiss him."

Neil did as he was told, making out with Joe so Morgan and Kate could watch. The women shared a secret smile and rubbed sinuously against Joe. Neil reached out, putting a hand on each of their waists, bracing himself for Mike, who entered in one long steady stroke.

He roared, praying he could find the strength to hold on though he knew the rest of the crew would cover for him if he faltered.

Mike began to pump into Neil. "No drama tonight. That's not what's happening here. Focus. My cock, your ass, everyone feeling good. That's all we're doing right now. Feeling. Feel this. Trust this."

Joe closed his eyes for a moment, then nodded before crushing his mouth to Neil's in a much more primal apology. The sort Mike had intended for him to give all along.

Morgan gasped and moaned. She loved watching Joe with the rest of the crew and she'd come harder for it later, Mike was sure of it. Here, he was every bit the foreman they expected him to be. Nothing felt more right than when they gave him control and he used it to bring them more pleasure than they ever could have imagined possible.

This was what he'd been made to do. And he damn well better not forget, same as he'd lectured them.

Mike leaned into Neil, sinking through the clenched rings of muscle guarding his tight ass. He worked inside bit by bit, easing through any resistance until his balls rested on the other guy's ass. Mike wrapped his fingers loosely around Neil's throat and used the grip to hold him steady as he began to ride.

There was something about the way they fit together that guaranteed Mike ended up stroking Neil's prostate when they fucked in this position. He usually saved it for last, drawing out Neil's ecstasy before setting him on fire. But not tonight. Not then. All he wanted was to take the man high, fast, so that he could fly with Devon, and James.

Besides, as much as self-control was something he prided himself on, even Mike had his limits. If he was going to fuck all four of the guys who'd also been his part-time lovers for the past two decades, he had to ration his own passion.

It didn't help when Kate leaned forward, running her hand along his chest and abdomen. He stretched his neck to capture her mouth and bucked harder into Neil, slapping his torso against the other guy's ass. His balls tapped the top of Neil's as he began to thrust harder. Kate devoured his grunt and groans, feeding him some whimpers of her own.

Enjoying both Kate and Neil, with the rest of the crew observing, Mike gave them everything he had. He reached beneath Neil, fishing for his cock. And when it bounced against his palm, he closed his hand, giving the guy something to rub into as Mike fucked him fast and hard.

The slippery fluid that coated his flesh made it clear he was enjoying what Mike did to him with every single shuttle of his hips. A steady string of curses interrupted Joe and Neil making out. And when Kate flicked the pad of her thumb across Mike's nipple, he rammed in deep then froze.

"Yeah. Yeah, that's all I can take." Neil whipped his

gaze to Devon and James. "Let me fuck them, now. Please, Mike. I have to come."

Mike cupped Neil's shoulders, helping him rise up. He wrapped his arms around the other guy and raked his teeth over Neil's neck, chuckling when Neil's ass clamped down on his dick. He held Neil steady as he withdrew, though they both gasped when the engorged head of his cock slipped free of Neil's hole.

"Go. Get them." Mike released Neil with a little shove in the right direction. Sometimes they were together, and sometimes he had to send them on their way, to do their own thing. Just like in life, the same was true here. He would do best to remember that come morning.

Neil crossed the space to where his husband and wife were nestled against the couch in a movement that reminded Mike of a wolf or a lion bounding toward its prey. He bowled into them and began to devour James even as he laid Devon flat on her back. In seconds, he was buried balls-deep in his wife while he made out with his husband and stroked the other man's rejuvenated hard-on.

James jerked as if he'd been struck by lightning, and within seconds lost control despite having come recently. His cock spurted, spraying Devon's hip and Neil's abdomen. At the sight, Devon's eyes rolled back. She shuddered and flew apart, wringing Neil's cock. He didn't stand a chance.

Neil bucked and shouted their names as he poured himself into Devon, overflowing her as his release mixed with James's inside her.

"I get it if you need to fuck Kate now," Joe said quietly as he kept up his slow massage of her from the inside out. "She's soaking wet and needs you."

"Like you don't?" Morgan asked her husband.

"I can wait." Kate sent him a wicked grin. "A couple minutes more."

"You think you're getting off the hook?" Mike stalked around Joe, then sank to his knees behind the other guy before raking his fingers along Joe's back from his shoulders to his ass.

"Just wasn't sure you could hold out that long." Joe rested his head on his wife's shoulder. Morgan stroked his hair from his forehead and kissed him there sweetly. "I should have known better. You're the most stubborn son of a bitch—"

Mike didn't bother arguing. Instead he showed his friend that he'd always have something left for him. He roared as he burrowed into Joe's lubed ass, possessing him with fierce thrusts he knew the other guy could not only handle, but would also love.

Of course, neither of them had much endurance left, already pushed to the brink of rapture by the sights and sounds of the people they loved enjoying each other so freely. And that was even before they tended to their wives, who had the power to amplify their desires.

Mike concentrated on making each stroke count, measured and fluid.

It wasn't long before Joe began to shake in his hold. So Mike pulled out and shoved Joe to his back, dislodging his hands from both Kate and Morgan. Joe grabbed for his wife, barely bouncing on the cushions once before he had her under him and had plunged inside her.

Mike had planned to fuck Kate while Joe did the same to Morgan, and while Kayla, Dave, James, Neil, and Dave watched on, but that's not exactly what happened.

Because first, Dave roared, then froze in Kayla before they both began to climax.

Their orgasms radiated through the room like a shockwave, setting Joe and Morgan off too.

And only then, with everyone else satisfied, did Mike advance on Kate. She met him smile for smile and held her arms open to him.

As they kissed, surprisingly tenderly, someone—James, he thought—cleaned off Mike's dick to ensure he was prepared for Kate. He muttered, "Thanks," without breaking eye contact with his wife.

Wanting to worship her and show her that this week had only made him love her that much more, he asked the crew for help. "I know we had our little party over the phone the other day, but Kayla wasn't there and, well, it's not the same when we're not in person."

"Are you asking us to help you and Kate celebrate the right way?" Neil asked.

"Yeah. Make this so good for her she never forgets tonight, please." Mike stroked the hair off her face and tucked it behind her ears as he laid her back against the cushions.

"I could never forget this," she promised as she looked around, reaching for Joe's hand on one side and Dave's on the other.

The guys didn't wait for Mike to beg, though. Instead, they kissed their wives to let them know they'd be back soon before kneeling in a ring around Kate.

Mike stayed upright on his knees as he lifted Kate's hips and found her center. He glided into her and sighed as he came home. The rest of the crew worshipped her, James leaning in to lick her clit as Mike fucked her, bumping into the other man's face on occasion. Dave and

Joe began laving her breasts, suckling them and stroking her all over while Joe made out with her.

Devon, Kayla, and Morgan huddled close to Mike. At first, he thought it was for a better look at what was happening, but then they started petting him, massaging his back and ass and rubbing his chest and abs while he made love to his wife.

He wished he really had the staying power they imagined, but there was no way either he or Kate could withstand their combined efforts. Especially not when someone slipped a slender finger in his ass.

But it was Kate, shattering around him, flying in the embrace of his friends while he did the same in the arms of hers, that sent him over the edge.

Mike shouted her name and something incomprehensible as he shot so hard and deep inside her he was worried he might have hurt her. His orgasm seemed endless, wringing him dry of both the physical and emotional energy that had been buzzing within him for weeks now.

And when the last of it drained from his body, their friends were there to settle them both next to each other and bring them gently back to reality.

The nine of them cuddled together, in their pairs and trio but also as one group, intertwined, impossible to break apart. Now or ever.

Mike felt lighter than he had in a while, because this had reminded him that no matter what else happened, they were bonded for life. He squeezed Kate to him and drifted long into the night.

And when people began to adjust themselves, find blankets, use the restroom, then settle in for a world-class slumber together, Dave stretched and yawned. Sleepily, he muttered his thoughts, which weren't so dissimilar to Mike's. "Maybe all of us should come out here and help with the Hot Rods project or even Giovanni's. We could go back, finish up this flip and be done in two weeks. We haven't made any commitments beyond that."

"Would you want us getting involved?" James asked without meeting Joe's gaze, as if he was afraid of being rejected.

Whoa. Mike hadn't realized the cracks in their foundation ran that deep. The caulk they'd reinforced them with tonight had been necessary and far too long coming. He wouldn't allow them to make that mistake again.

Fortunately, Joe shut that down fast. "Of course I would love it if you were here. I didn't dare ask. Or even hope... Would you really do that? For me?"

"Yeah, of course," Neil answered in a heartbeat, James and Devon doing the same.

"My only concern is leaving Kayla for that long." Dave ran his hand along her back lovingly.

She cleared her throat. "You'll have an awesome time. I can hold down the fort at Bare Natural. It's our peak season, so I can't stay way for long. It's bad enough we shut down this weekend."

Dave winced and hugged her tight. "I'm sorry, babe. You're right. I wasn't thinking."

"I'm serious." She kissed his cheek. "I can handle it. The crew needs you more than I do right now."

That wasn't going to fly. Mike could already tell. There was no way in hell Dave was going to abandon Kayla and putting him in position to choose them over her would be as stressful as it had been for Joe. It had nearly ripped him apart.

"Let's sleep on it. We can worry about the future tomorrow." Mike looked around the room at the eight other men and women tangled together. He didn't want anything to ruin the peace they'd found in each other's arms.

There would be plenty of time to fuck things up in the morning.

13

————

The problem with waiting for tomorrow is sometimes it never comes. Or worse, it comes but there are so many other unexpected shit-storms swirling around that you can't deal with the ones left over from the day before. It had been that kind of year for Mike and the rest of the Powertools crew. Hell, for most of the world, he figured.

He should have known the next morning would bring more bad news.

Agonizing devastation.

And that there wouldn't be anything he could do to stop his friends from getting leveled by it.

He was lying in their makeshift bed, wrapped in Kate and several someone elses when a buzzing phone roused him from sleep. At first he swatted in the direction of his nightstand before hearing Neil's *oof* as his hand connected with some exposed bit of the other guy. "Sorry, dude."

Mike blinked and scrubbed his eyes. In the background, someone was talking. "No. We're not home.

We're out of state at a wedding. The resort is closed. Empty. It's... It's what?"

He was still trying to make sense of where he was and what was going on when a haunting wail cut through the early-morning peace. They probably hadn't been asleep for more than a couple hours, the stars still lighting the woods outside as the sun peeked above the horizon.

"What the fuck?" Mike sat bolt upright, that mournful cry sending icy spears through his guts. He'd heard that noise once before, a long time ago. It was Kayla.

She'd sounded exactly that way when they'd found out that Dave had been in a near-fatal car accident, before they knew he would ultimately pull through.

He scrambled toward her in the dark, going purely by instinct in the direction of the sound.

The rest of the crew was moving too. Dave, of course, was already there, gripping Kayla's arms and holding her up when she would have collapsed if left on her own. "What's happened? What is it?"

"That was the police." Kayla swallowed hard, as if she might be sick. Her usually pale skin was nearly translucent, making her tattoos seem even more vivid despite the early morning light. "There's a wildfire. A bad one. Bare Natural is burning."

She began to hyperventilate, breathing so raggedly and fast that Mike was afraid she'd pass out.

"Oh no. No!" Morgan was there beside her in a moment, wrapping her arms around Kayla's waist and hugging her tight even as Dave surrounded them both in his arms. He attempted to shield them from as much pain as he could. He rocked Kayla and promised her things were going to be all right.

Mike hoped he wasn't lying.

In the meantime, Joe fished in a basket on the side of the couch and came up with a remote. He turned the lights on very low, so dim they were almost orange. Mike cringed as the group was cast in an amber glow that made him think of sitting by a fireplace. Any other time it would have been soothing, reminding him of the huge hearth they often spread out in front of at Kayla and Dave's cabin in the woods. Right then, it sent shivers up his spine.

Kate was there, plastered against his side. He clung to her even as he looked around at the rest of his crew doing the same with their partners. Joe flipped on the news and there, in horrific high-definition, was the truth.

The entire mountaintop where Kayla's resort was perched, overlooking the lake in the distance, was engulfed in flames. This wasn't a matter of containment or putting it out quickly...it was an inferno eating everything in its path.

Kayla began sobbing, as did James and several other of their friends.

Mike stared in shock. All he could think to say was, "Thank God you're not there. I'm so grateful the resort was closed this weekend for the wedding. There are no guests, right? No one up there at all, is there?"

Dave shook his head over top of Kayla's. She was too distraught to hear Mike's question, never mind respond. Mike thought of his children and how they'd stayed in those woods a mere two days before. Black smoke poured from the blaze.

He plopped onto his ass and prayed, grateful that at least they were all here. All safe.

The reporter droned on in the background. "...believe to have been caused by a lightning strike in the storm that passed through early this morning..."

Mike had been there, loving his crew, hoping he was building some kind of future for them, when in reality everything that Kayla and Dave had worked toward for so long was going up in smoke. How the fuck was he going to make this right?

Kayla bolted to her feet, looking for something to wear even if it was her little black party dress, which seemed entirely out of place in their current reality. "I have to go back. I have to do...*something*."

They all knew there was absolutely nothing she was going to be able to do to save Bare Natural, but no one was going to stand in her way either. Mike got to his feet and pulled on his jeans. But standing there, bare-chested and barefooted, he realized pretty damn quick that this was a turning point for them.

Because Joe couldn't leave. And Kayla couldn't stay.

So what about him? Kate? Devon, James, and Neil?

Where did that leave them?

Mike stood taller, taking charge when everyone else turned to him. He pointed at James. "You three with them. They're going to need help and someone to drive. Kayla's too upset and Dave should focus on her."

Neil, Devon, and James were already getting dressed and searching for the small suitcase they'd packed for their weekend trip.

"And you?" Neil asked.

Kate looked to Mike too, worrying her lower lip between her teeth.

"We're going to stay here and keep things on track with Joe and the Hot Rods project. Is that okay with everyone?" He looked around the room. Kayla hadn't even heard him. Dave was focused entirely on her, wrapping her in a blanket when she began to shake uncontrollably.

"I guess it'll have to be." Neil blew out a breath and Devon *tsked* at him.

"Quit that." She glared at her husband. "There isn't a choice. Don't make it harder on him. Yes, of course it will be fine. Do what you have to, Mike. We will too. No matter what happens, we'll always be a crew. You showed us that last night. Things might be...different...for a while. Until we can figure this out for good. But we *will* do that. Right?"

"Yeah. Exactly." Mike hugged her. "Keep the guys in line and let me know if you need anything, no matter how small, for the Powertools project or Bare Natural, okay?"

"You know I will." She went up on her tiptoes and kissed his cheek. "Now, we better get on the road."

There was a flurry of motion, people putting on clothes, even ones that might not have been their own, taking turns in the bathroom, and gathering the rest of their belongings. In under ten minutes, which was kind of a miracle for a group their size, they were marching out the door, one by one.

Dave escorted Kayla, who stumbled toward the van like a zombie, his thick arm protective as it curled around her shoulders and kept her tucked to his body. He opened the door and helped her inside. Her soft crying broke Mike's heart as he stood in the driveway, still without his shoes.

Hugs were exchanged, Mike clinging to James until they were the last two holding up the group's departure. He held on to the doorframe and leaned into the van as James settled into place. "Drive safe. I'm so sorry. So sorry."

Not only for Kayla and Dave, but for each of them. For having to say goodbye like this and for having to split up, no matter for how long. It went against everything he held dear, and yet there wasn't anything he could do to stop it.

"It's not your fault," Dave said quietly.

"I still hate it." Mike took a deep breath, then said, "Call us when you get there."

He shut the door, which rang with a finality that broke his heart in the still morning. The sun now peeked through the trees, about to go to war with the mist swirling around the trunks. It should have been a special day, a sacred one, and instead it was a nightmare come to life.

Devon—who was driving—gave them one final wave, then looked in the rearview mirror, backing out of the driveway and setting them onto the road home. Without him. Without Kate. Without Joe or Morgan or any of their kids.

Joe's phone rang as half of their crew accelerated in the wrong direction, away from them. Every instinct Mike had urged him to charge after them even though he knew that wasn't the right thing to do.

"Hey, Eli." Joe's voice was shredded, nearly as much as Mike's guts from the events of the past half hour. His family had probably seen the news on TV, too.

"Huh? You haven't heard? Then what are you calling me for this early?" Joe paused, then said, "You know what? It's better if we come over. We'll fill you in and you can do the same. See you in a few."

Mike didn't really feel like going anywhere, unless it was to chase down the half of the crew disappearing around a bend in the woods. But he figured he might as well stick with Joe and learn to rely on his friend's family as if they were his own.

Right now, they could use all the help they could get.

14

Mike still couldn't believe it had happened. The fire. The fracturing of Powertools.

But here he was, with Kate, Joe, and Morgan, while Neil, James, Devon, Dave, and Kayla were on their way home. This time for good.

Eli, Tom, and Ms. Brown fussed over the four crew members as they filled them in on the tragedy that had struck Bare Natural, and specifically Kayla. Her brother Gavyn was married to Ms. Brown's daughter Amber. The more Mike thought about it, the more he realized they were really one big intertwined family.

He should have recognized that before. But in crises like these, it became obvious.

Ms. Brown made tea and coffee, and offered them breakfast, though no one had the appetite for it right then. Mike kept hearing Kayla's wail echo through his memory and knew he'd have nightmares where she cried out and he couldn't reach her, just like he couldn't at that moment.

"Well, shit." Eli ran his hands through his hair. "This is terrible timing but..."

Joe narrowed his eyes. "Yeah, why did you call earlier if you didn't know about the fire yet?"

Eli looked to his dad, who nodded. "Go ahead. No reason to let bad news overshadow the good."

"If you have something positive to talk about, we'll take it." Kate rested her cheek on Mike's shoulder. He ran his hand up and down her arm. If he hadn't had her by his side, this morning would have been far worse. So he concentrated on being grateful for that at least.

"All right. Giovanni must have stopped by after the wedding and stuck this in the door. I threw it on the counter when we got in because I was focused on other things." Eli slid a packet of papers, ensconced in a black plastic sliding bar report cover across the table to Joe and Mike. "I hope you don't mind, but I peeked at it after...you know...and I thought you'd want to see it right away. Honestly, I couldn't sleep after I looked at it, but I waited as long as I could to call Joe. I figured if you were still knocked out you would ignore me."

Joe opened the cover, then shut it. Then opened it again.

His jaw dropped before he handed the plan to Mike.

There, right at the top of the page, was a proposed budget of three point two five million dollars for Giovanni's shop and a connected entertainment complex including a small tattoo-themed hotel, a couple restaurants, shops, an ink museum, and other attractions. *Holy shit.*

Their potential cut alone had a hell of a lot of zeros after it.

"We'd have to flip five years' worth of houses to make a profit like that." Joe pinched the bridge of his nose. "But I can't do this. Not now. Not by myself. I'd need Mike as my partner, at the very least, to even think about accepting a job on that scale."

"We can't desert Dave and Kayla. Especially not now that they're going to need so much help to clean up and rebuild." Mike scrubbed his hand over his face. Why the hell had the perfect opportunity shown up at exactly the wrong time?

"Listen to me, boys." Tom cleared his throat. "Sometimes we get so used to how things are, we don't see how they can be different, so here's an idea for you..."

Ms. Brown put her hand in Tom's and smiled at them as if she already knew what he would say.

"Maybe the best way you can help Kayla and Bare Natural right now is to take this deal and make it work." Tom shushed their objections. "Hear me out. I know she has insurance, but there's going to be miles of red tape and it's going to take time to sort through. Months before they can be up and running at the same capacity again. Next season if she's lucky. The advance from this project would be enough to get them started. Hell, you could even afford to pay Dave, Devon, Neil, and James's salary as Powertools to work on the reconstruction. And as good as you both are at construction shit, being able to give them that—the gift of time and financial independence while they're healing and rebuilding—*that* might be the most valuable thing you can do for your friends."

Mike felt the air whoosh out of his lungs.

Because Uncle Tom was absolutely right.

Kayla and Dave, along with James, Devon, and Neil, would benefit more than even Joe and him from the opportunity sitting there in front of them. All they had to do was accept it and work their asses off, together, to make the project a success. It wasn't a given. It was going to require negotiations, long nights, a mountain of stress, and learning lots of new shit, but for the first time in a while...Mike felt a spark of excitement at the idea.

Tackling the challenge with Joe could be exactly what he needed to feel useful, and to help forge a way forward for the entire Powertools crew.

"Would you want to do that?" Joe asked Mike, as if afraid of the answer. "Come on board as the foreman of a new, much bigger operation?"

"No way," Mike instinctively objected.

Joe's face fell, Eli looked away, and Tom gathered Ms. Brown closer.

"What I mean is if we do this, we're going in equals. Partners. Co-foremen." Mike stared straight into Joe's eyes. "You're going to be every bit as responsible as me if this thing tanks."

Although he knew it wouldn't. Not if they teamed up like they had so many times before. This time on a much grander scale.

"Oh. Right." Joe seemed shocked, but nodded slowly as a grin spread across Eli's face. The garage owner clapped his cousin on the back. "Then you're considering it?"

Mike couldn't believe it, but he was. No, he'd already decided. So long as it was okay with Kate. "What do you think, babe?"

Her eyes were big as she looked up at him then around the room. He could feel her pulse racing in her wrist, where his fingers rested on her soft skin. "My scouting trip with Ollie last week was incredible. If you want to do this, I could maybe take a few gambles of my own. I think it could work. For everyone."

"We have an extra bedroom and plenty of space." Joe looked to her, an expression on his face that looked like Mike's felt. Like he was stunned but thrilled things were falling into place even if they hated how it had come to be. A dazed sort of euphoria that had come with a hell of a steep price tag.

"Our kids would love spending more time together this summer." Morgan smiled at Kate. "And you won't have to go through your pregnancy alone. I'll be here. Sally's experiencing the same stuff too, and Joy and Amber have done it recently. You'll have plenty of support."

Kate put her hand on Mike's and squeezed. She looked up at him and nodded.

"I guess it looks like we're moving in..." Mike smiled at Joe and added, "...*partner*."

Tom lifted Ms. Brown, who kicked her feet playfully, and spun her around, while Eli squeezed Joe's shoulder. He looked across the table at Kate and Mike and said, "Welcome home."

The only thing that could have made the moment better was if the rest of the crew was there with them. But Mike figured they were going to have to work on accepting that fate had other plans for them. No matter what happened next, things would never be the same again.

And that might be okay.

Kate turned to him, framed his face with her hands, and kissed him softly. "As long as we're together, us and the kids, everything will be all right. And I think it's going to be much better than simply okay in time. Maybe this is how it's supposed to be."

Mike decided to trust her because she'd never been wrong before. So he pulled Kate into his lap and wrapped her and their unborn baby in his protective hold, ready to embark on a new adventure.

142

If you'd like to start at the very beginning with the Powertools Crew, you can download a discounted boxset of the first six books HERE.

Yes, know it says complete series but I wrote a seventh book more recently and haven't gotten around to updating the boxset yet, sorry!

You can find the seventh Powertools book, More the Merrier, HERE.

If you missed out on the Powertools: Hot Rods series, you can buy all eight books in a discounted single-volume boxset by clicking HERE.

To read more about the Hot Rides gang, starting with Quinn, Trevon, and Devra's story, Wild Ride, click HERE.

CLAIM A $5 GIFT CERTIFICATE

Jayne is so sure you will love her books, she'd like you to try any one of your choosing for free. Claim your $5 gift certificate by signing up for her newsletter. You'll also learn about freebies, new releases, extras, appearances, and more!

www.jaynerylon.com/newsletter

WHAT WAS YOUR FAVORITE PART?

Did you enjoy this book? If so, please leave a review and tell your friends about it. Word of mouth and online reviews are immensely helpful and greatly appreciated.

JAYNE'S SHOP

Check out Jayne's online shop for autographed print books, direct download ebooks, reading-themed apparel up to size 5XL, mugs, tote bags, notebooks, Mr. Rylon's wood (you'll have to see it for yourself!) and more.
www.jaynerylon.com/shop

LISTEN UP!

The majority of Jayne's books are also available in audio format on Audible, Amazon and iTunes.

ABOUT THE AUTHOR

Jayne Rylon is a *New York Times* and *USA Today* bestselling author who has sold more than one million books. She has received numerous industry awards including the Romantic Times Reviewers' Choice Award for Best Indie Erotic Romance and the Swirl Award, which recognizes excellence in diverse romance. She is an Honor Roll member of the Romance Writers of America. Her stories used to begin as daydreams in seemingly endless business meetings, but now she is a full time author, who employs the skills she learned from her straight-laced corporate existence in the business of writing. She lives in Ohio with her husband, the infamous Mr. Rylon, and their cat, Frodo. When she can escape her purple office, she loves to travel the world, avoid speeding tickets in her beloved Sky, SCUBA dive, hunt Pokemon, and–of course–read.

Jayne Loves To Hear From Readers
www.jaynerylon.com
contact@jaynerylon.com
PO Box 10, Pickerington, OH 43147

facebook.com/jaynerylon

twitter.com/JayneRylon

instagram.com/jaynerylon

youtube.com/jaynerylonbooks

bookbub.com/profile/jayne-rylon

amazon.com/author/jaynerylon

ALSO BY JAYNE RYLON

4-EVER

A New Adult Reverse Harem Series

4-Ever Theirs

4-Ever Mine

EVER AFTER DUET

Reverse Harem Featuring Characters From The 4-Ever Series

Fourplay

Fourkeeps

EVER & ALWAYS DUET

Reverse Harem Featuring Characters from the 4-Ever and Ever After Duets

Four Money

Four Love

POWERTOOLS: THE ORIGINAL CREW

Five Guys Who Get It On With Each Other & One Girl. Enough Said?

Kate's Crew

Morgan's Surprise

Kayla's Gift

Devon's Pair

Nailed to the Wall

Hammer it Home

More the Merrier *NEW*

POWERTOOLS: HOT RODS

Powertools Spin Off. Keep up with the Crew plus...

Seven Guys & One Girl. Enough Said?

King Cobra

Mustang Sally

Super Nova

Rebel on the Run

Swinger Style

Barracuda's Heart

Touch of Amber

Long Time Coming

POWERTOOLS: HOT RIDES

Powertools and Hot Rods Spin Off.

Menage and Motorcycles

Wild Ride

Slow Ride

Hard Ride

Joy Ride

Rough Ride

POWERTOOLS: RETURN OF THE CREW

The original crew is back with more steamy menage stories!

Screwed

Drilled

Grind

Pound

MEN IN BLUE

Hot Cops Save Women In Danger

Night is Darkest

Razor's Edge

Mistress's Master

Spread Your Wings

Wounded Hearts

Bound For You

DIVEMASTERS

Sexy SCUBA Instructors By Day, Doms On A Mega-Yacht By Night

Going Down

Going Deep

Going Hard

STANDALONE

Menage

Middleman

Nice & Naughty

Contemporary

Where There's Smoke

Report For Booty

COMPASS BROTHERS

Modern Western Family Drama Plus Lots Of Steamy Sex

Northern Exposure

Southern Comfort

Eastern Ambitions

Western Ties

COMPASS GIRLS

Daughters Of The Compass Brothers Drive Their Dads Crazy And Fall In Love

Winter's Thaw

Hope Springs

Summer Fling

Falling Softly

COMPASS BOYS

Sons Of The Compass Brothers Fall In Love

Heaven on Earth

Into the Fire

Still Waters

Light as Air

PLAY DOCTOR

Naughty Sexual Psychology Experiments Anyone?

Dream Machine

Healing Touch

RED LIGHT

A Hooker Who Loves Her Job

Complete Red Light Series Boxset

FREE - Through My Window - FREE

Star

Can't Buy Love

Free For All

PICK YOUR PLEASURES

Choose Your Own Adventure Romances!

Pick Your Pleasure

Pick Your Pleasure 2

RACING FOR LOVE

MMF Menages With Race-Car Driver Heroes

Complete Series Boxset

Driven

Shifting Gears

PARANORMALS

Vampires, Witches, And A Man Trapped In A Painting

Paranormal Double Pack Boxset

Picture Perfect

Reborn

PENTHOUSE PLEASURES

Naughty Manhattanite Neighbors Find Kinky Love

Taboo

Kinky

Sinner

Mentor

ROAMING WITH THE RYLONS

Non-fiction Travelogues about Jayne & Mr. Rylon's Adventures

Australia and New Zealand